The Queen of Ice & Stone

by

C. M. Hano

Hearts Of Dalaria, Book Two

Cover Art by *Lea Schizas*

The Wild Rose Press, Inc.
PO Box 708
Adams Basin, NY 14410-0708
Visit us at www.thewildrosepress.com

Publishing History
First Edition, 2025
Trade Paperback ISBN 978-1-5092-5986-1
Digital ISBN 978-1-5092-5987-8

Hearts Of Dalaria, Book Two
Published in the United States of America

Dedication

To my sister in arms.

Part One: Ice

Chapter One

Rowland

I hate being summoned.

I must attend to a drunk person now, so I have to pause my duties as the lord of this kingdom. It's frustrating that our world is crumbling, and we cannot fix it. Zoldir, unlike the rumored Orion Fortress, is a small castle with four ivory towers. These towers provide a perfect vantage point for our archers to watch over the small wasteland inhabited by docile people. The pointed crimson flags that bear the symbol of Zoldir—a golden hatchet—protrude from a metal post on each tower. The harsh environment and the missing concrete slabs leave the palace vulnerable to the scorching heat of the land. The walk from my chambers to the throne room is as mundane as the rest of the place. Each column has slim oil lanterns that dimly glow, making it difficult to see at night. And during the day, it highlights the cracks in the fixtures and walls. On either side of the corridor are statues of past monarchs dating back to the creation of Zoldir–my ancestor, Richard Kawthorne.

I love my home, but since the death of my parents ten years ago—a disease of the heart, is what the physicians called it, has fallen further into ruin.

The large doors make a loud noise as I enter

through double-wide oak tree doors. The guards swung them open with too much force, and the weight knocked them into the walls. The ceiling tremors cause particles to filter into the humid air.

"As if our castle didn't need enough repairs, why not add more cracks," I snap.

"Apologies—"

"I'm not in the mood for excuses," I interrupt. A chalice comes flying between us, aimed directly at Hobbes Froshier–advisor to the king. "Hobbes, you pathetic, useless creature of a human being. I command you to fetch Rowland."

I sighed upon hearing the slurring in each word he spoke.

Looking toward the timid advisor, the golden locks of his shake with the trembling fear racing through his petite body. "Sire—"

"No. Not another word from you, or I will have your tongue removed," Gregor exclaims, pointing a burley finger at the man.

"Hello, brother; what do you need from me now?" Gregor's amber eyes darted to mine. His fierce gaze falters as a smile forms just beneath his beard.

"Rowland." He stumbled from his throne, his tunic rolling up, showing off his round gut. I move closer, ready to catch him if he falls down the three small steps of the raised platform…again.

"Easy. I wouldn't want you to break your neck," I tease, but he narrows his brows in confusion. "It was a joke, Gregor."

He scoffs and walks over to the long table at the center, gripping the steel metal of a decanter, and pours red wine into another chalice. "Rowland, I need you to plan an invasion."

"What?" He has never suggested anything as ludicrous as this, even in his worst inebriated state.

He finished the wine, small droplets running down his beard, staining his tunic, and he turned to look at me again. "I didn't stutter. We will be invading Orion Fortress and stealing their dragon heart."

"Have you lost your gods-damned mind?"

"Watch your tone, boy. You may be twenty-five and grown, but I am still your king."

"I won't argue that point," I said, knowing there was no use in continuing my interrogation into whatever was going on inside his diluted brain. "But there's one problem—we can't get across the wall."

"We'll find a way," he snapped back. I glared at him, and he rolled his eyes. "I can practically see the steam coming from your ears," he said. "Ask your questions, Rowland."

"Why are we invading a realm we don't even know exists? As far as we know, Orion Fortress is some made-up place to make the possibility of leaving this wasteland for a world of wonder," I asked him sardonically while narrowing my eyes.

He sighed heavily and returned to his throne to plop down. "The Grand Council has informed me that the Zikyr's ember is fading."

"That's not possible. That magic has been in use since Grandsire Richard was king." I've only seen it a couple of times, and when I did, it seemed quaint. It was radiant and golden. It was more beautiful than any gem I'd ever seen. Not that we have many of those, either.

"If we don't find a way to light it again, our world

will cease to exist. You know this place was created by magic, and we will die without it. So, all the food and necessary resources to survive will be gone. Each one of us will die of starvation or kill each other over the last slice of bread. Do you want our subjects to go through this?"

He's trying to manipulate me again. I go quiet as I ponder what he said, knowing he is right and not wanting this to happen. I devise an idea. "What if we send a messenger hawk over the border? They fly high enough to cross over it. I'm sure it will work."

"I've sent five, and each has been met with silence."

"There has to be another way. They have never wronged us."

"The only thing you will be doing is finding a way for humans to cross that barrier without being vaporized by its magic. Do not return to me until you have that answer."

I turn on my heel at his dismissal, hating how he treats me like I am just another citizen. "And, Rowland…" I look over my shoulder. "If you think we will get out of this using your diplomatic tongue, you're highly mistaken."

****

Kaleigh

There is something serene about being in the forest.

The feather tip of my arrow tickles my cheek as I pull back hard on the fine horse hair of Shadow Strike–the only compound bow I will ever trust to reach its target. A warm breath kisses the back of my neck, and I ignore it as the buck grazes.

Inhale, exhale, release.

My muscles ease the moment the arrow flies, sinking into the chest cavity of my prize.

"Well done, Your Highness." Tristian's lips graze my neck, his words sending heat through my veins, causing my core to clench. "But…" His hands move to my hips, gripping them firmly before pressing himself into me. "…you need to work on not letting things distract you."

I spin on my heel, bow discarded on the ground, before my hand shoots out to grip his neck. Forcing his back to the trunk of the tree, I reach for the top of his trousers, unbuttoning them to grip his hard length. I stroke him up and down, keeping my lips a breath away while I work him into a frenzy.

"Beg," I demand. His cobalt eyes are burning with lust, his grip tightening. I know I'll have bruises in the morning.

"Please." He groans. "I'll do anything, princess."

My lips crush against his, my pace increasing as my pussy became wet, and the need to feel him inside of me sent me over the edge of my control. Our tongues clash, and I break only momentarily to say, "Kneel before me and show me how much you worship me."

His knees impact the grass, hands moving to lift the skirts of my hunting dress. I grip his hair tightly as his tongue licks me from taunt to clit, a moan escaping me. My hips begin rolling, and I ride his face into oblivion. It's not enough. I push him onto his back, straddling him and sinking. We both groan, and I pick up the pace, searching for another orgasm while his thumb circles my bundle of nerves. Tristian may be a manservant, but he knows how to please me. I don't relinquish control as I pick up the pace, my heart thumping in my ears, my vision going spotty, and I feel it in my core. My pussy clenches tight around him, and we explode, his seed spewing into me while I dig into his shoulders.

Our chests rise and fall, sweat gleaming on both of our brows, and I fall forward, resting my head on him while we both come down from our moment of ecstasy.

"I wish we didn't have to hide," he whispered into my ear, fingers caressing my back up and down. I move from on top of him, stand, and turn away, using the inseam of the skirt to clean myself before marching off to find my kill. He is always like this after we have sex, wanting to talk about the emotions of our relationship, and I don't have the heart to tell him I'm using him for sex and that nothing will ever come of this. He's attractive, tall, broad-frame, with flawless skin and unique silver-white hair cropped above his ears, but he isn't the man I see myself marrying or ruling Orion with.

The buck is barely breathing when I reach it. Its large black lids are half-closed as the god of death arrives to reap his soul. I kneel before him, pulling my arrow from his chest; his ears twitch in response, confirming that he is at the end. I place the gore-covered arrow on the forest floor behind me, a hand on his snout before reciting, "I humbly thank you for this gift you have given my people. Your fur will be used for warmth, bones for protection, and meat for hunger."

I place a small kiss and wait until his final breath exhales.

With the game secured to Ivy's saddle, I check my long braid for leaves and sweat from my brow or evidence of extra events that occurred today and gulp water from my waterskin.

"Do you ever wonder if we'll ever talk about it?" he asked. I keep my back to him and the tip of my waterskin to my lips, pretending to drink so I don't have to answer. I realize that avoiding it is wrong, but I'm not ready. He'll keep asking if I don't say something, and we'll have to stop our little tryst.

"We've been friends since we were fifteen, for ten years." I begin packing my waterskin back in its place before turning to look at him. Aside from the obvious dirt on his red tunic and brown trousers, his appearance is impeccable, which is typical for a hunt. "And friends are what we will remain."

His eyes flash, and I know I've hurt him. He goes to speak, but a booming voice interrupts him before he gets a chance. "Princess?" Sir Palmer said. "The king and queen have requested that you return to the palace immediately."

"Princess," Tristian started. I held my hand up to stop him.

"Conversation is over. Duty calls," I say dismissively before mounting my stallion and trotting toward my uncle.

****

"Kaleigh, come in, darling." Queen Alina regally gestures with a gloved hand.

"Your Grace, I thought I was meeting with both of you?" I inquire.

"Your father is tending to business elsewhere," she quips.

"Well, let me hear it." I know this will end in a lecture. She despises my love for hunting and exploration.

"Thank you, Kaleigh. I just want to know when you leave. You are twenty-five and the future queen of our land. There is so much you need to learn. And your sister is nearing her twenty-third name day. If she sees you getting away with skipping out on all these lessons and council meetings, then she'll assume it's okay for her to follow in your footsteps. I need a daughter who is willing to become a queen. A wife and possibly a mother."

I suppress the urge to cut my eyes at her repetitive speech. She closes the short distance between us, stopping just a foot in front of me before looking at me from head to toe. Father says I am the spitting image of her. We both have waist-length, thick brown curls, dark blue-green eyes, and fair skin. Our stature is small, although I have been building muscles over the years since I started training when I was five. My mother is beautiful in her fiftieth year.

"Well, no pressure, right? What else do I need to know? You and Father are fine." I smile, reassuring her that I have no plans of becoming queen yet.

"When you are ready, you will know everything." She hugged me before taking her leave, not allowing me to speak further on the issue of my birthright.

****

The garden has always been a tranquil place where I can think about my day and let my future thoughts drift away. I admire the architecture of small stone structures filled with blooming flowers. Roses, tulips, and lilacs, named after the willow trees in the forest, give a blissful aroma. The Willow Well Garden is at the center of the courtyard. The White Sun's beams shine down on a rounded fixture of varying materials. Filled with clear water, I can see my reflection in the pool and wonder if it represents me.

"Princess, am I disturbing you?" Hilda, the royal healer, interrupts my quiet. But I was expecting her. Just as I always do when I return from a hunt.

"Place it over there," I command without looking at her. The tray clinks against the stone and her footsteps recede. "Hilda, I do appreciate your continued discretion."

"Of course, Your Highness." I wait until the doors shut before picking up my steaming tea. Pennyroyal doesn't taste that great, but it will prevent conception. After drinking it, I sit at the edge of the well and run my fingers through it, sighing as the cool smoothness glides along my skin.

"I suppose it's time to head to bed," I speak out loud, taking my hand from the water, but it doesn't move. What the hell? I tug again, but the resistance is stronger. My heart pounds in my chest as it squeezes the more I tug, but the water won't release its hold. I feel my body falling forward until the water surrounds me. I scream, but it can't be heard. My throat is on fire, and I struggle to swim to the surface.

"Princess Kaleigh," a soft voice calls my name. Like a siren, it soothed me. The panic fades, and a bubble of light forms in front of me. I swim toward it, praying it is the surface. Until I see an image. It's blurred at first; I blink a few times, and it clears.

"I'll be seeking an audience with the princess." A man I've never seen before with black hair and brown eyes is speaking with someone. The image shifts to him marching in the forbidden forest. His face comes closer until his eyes lock with mine.

I snap awake, coughing and inhaling air. Looking around, I'm still in the garden but not wet. I've heard that the herb causes hallucinations, but this is the third time I've taken it, and I've never had any side effects.

Rushing out of the garden, I hurry down the hall to the right and straight through the doors to my chambers. My brain is fogged until something hits my head, and I look and find my little sister shouting at me with her hair half-combed. The utensil was discarded at my feet. "Did you just throw your brush at me?"

"You walked in without knocking!" Abbygale yelled as I closed and locked her doors.

"I need to talk." My somber tone had the anger receding from her face.

Chapter Two

Rowland

The Obelisk Library is our most beautiful building. It comprises large quartz stones that comprise most of the building's structure. It is difficult to see through the misted windows. And I've started welcoming the smell of old parchments and dust every time I step through the oak door.

This is where I will find my answers. Where I find my peace.

Ivan Froshier, Hobbes's grandsire, greets me with a smile and a bow and asks the same question each time I enter this building. "Welcome, Your Highness. What knowledge do you seek on this fine day?"

His long white beard sways against the floor, and his rounded spectacles slide down his pointed nose with each word he speaks. "Hello, Ivan. I am looking for an answer on how to reach the king on the other side of the barrier."

"Ah, follow me." He gestured, and I followed.

We pass shelves lined with scrolls and different novels from the beginning of Zoldir's time. There is so much knowledge I would spend a lifetime soaking up if I had the time. If Gregor wasn't a drunk.

"Have you seen it?" I ask him as he shuffles through the back shelf, muttering incoherent words under his breath.

He continues scrummaging until his fingers brush against a large spine wrapped in leather. Pulling it from the shelf, he walks to a round table, and I watch as he places the book down. It's a dusty old leather book with a bronze brushed letter 'D' emblazoned upon the center of the cover.

"This is the book of Dalaria. Everything you want to know about this world will be revealed there."

A spark of electricity buzzed against my fingertips as I grazed the center. "Thank you."

"Of course." He bowed and turned to walk away, but I stopped him with another question.

"Do you know what it will be like? The other side?"

He smirked. "In my experience, letting others figure things out for themselves is best. My journey will be different from yours, my prince."

A man with a mysterious past. I can respect him for not wanting to share it. I know I never talk about mine.

I turn my attention back to the book and open it. Passing by Zoldir, I stopped on the next chapter titled "Hollow Realm" and read the description: 'Black soot bellows out of cracks in the ground, creating a thick toxic air to anyone who breathes.'

"Sounds like a dreadful place. I won't be visiting you anytime soon," I muttered to myself and flipped to the next chapter.

Orion Fortress: 'Beware of this place, disguised in beauty, built on betrayal and the blood of many.'

Interesting. How can a place be disguised in beauty but built on blood? I flip to the next page, hoping to find more than cryptic descriptions and slam my hand down on a blank page.

"Gods!" My voice echoed through the empty library, and I palm my face in embarrassment. "Apologies, Ivan."

He muttered something I couldn't understand, and then I looked back at the page.

Ready to slam it shut, I paused when something unbelievable happened.

The page started to glow, and fresh writing appeared. I read it out loud following the exact words written. "When you need to know, the light ahead will show the path you will find in due time."

Gods. This is weird, exhilarating, and impossible.

"Ivan?" I looked around for the librarian, but he seemed to have disappeared from me. "Cool it, Rowland. You're just freaking out over magic. And now, talking to yourself in the third person."

I scrub my hand down my face and close the book. Thinking it's best to leave magic where it belongs.

Lost.

Standing, looking to see where Ivan had gone, I noticed a black door, slightly hidden between two towering shelves of books. Approaching it, the handle is a golden crescent, and an eerie feeling passes from it into me, causing a shiver to race up and down my spine.

"It's just a door. What could be hiding behind it?"

I reach out, gripping the cold steel lever, push forward, and am immediately met by a lonely corridor.

"I'm not dead yet. Ivan, are you back here?" My voice echoes and then disappears into the void. "I'm coming inside."

The ground beneath my feet crunches, and a gust of wind almost knocks me over. My skin is freezing, and a cloud of smoke is created with every exhale. "Nothing against old people, but you sure love the cold….maybe too cold," I state low enough so he can't hear me.

At the end of the corridor, I find myself standing in front of another blackened door. "What is this? Is it some kind of extension? Ivan, we need to talk about how much time you have on your hands if you're building more parts…and your incredible strength."

I push through this time.

In a flurry of freezing air, sharp needles poked from green tree branches, and white particles flowed from a blackened sky, causing me to halt my steps. Looking around, I see the ground beneath my feet is a glistening pearl color.

"Ivan?" I ask out loud. "Where are you? There is no way this is a part of Zoldir." When nothing but silence greets me, I turn around but see nothing but the forest behind me. "Where's the door? Where's the fucking door?"

Panic seized me, my heart rate increased, and the surrounding world closed in on me. "Deep breaths. Deep breaths."

Slowly calming myself, I feel a cold gust kiss my heated flesh, helping me gain control of my anxiety attack.

I rub my arms, quickly realizing that if I don't get out of this crazy weather, I may freeze to death.

In the distance, I spot a single orange light and what looks like a road. Walking up to the flicker, I noticed two signs, one pointed toward Orion Fortress and the other toward Sumter. "I guess that answers my question then. We've gotten ourselves across the barrier. The answer was in the library, after all. Great! Now I'm talkin' to myself again."

The road isn't made from the same materials we use back home. It is made up of cobblestones that surprisingly complement the land's beauty. The smell of the air is unfamiliar, but it's nice and sweet, like Mother's perfume. I sigh at the memory of her. "Gone but not forgotten."

She and Father died of natural causes, according to the palace healers. But they were so young, too young, in my opinion. I would like to think Gregor felt the same way, but each time I bring them up, he tries to fight me. I gave up and turned to my books while he drowned his sorrows.

With each gust of wind, I couldn't stop rubbing my arms, trying to warm them up. I'm not used to these freezing temperatures.

This place may be more beautiful than Zoldir, but much more miserable.

A glimmer of hope started to rise within me the further I traveled, and then, out of nowhere, I came across a bridge that crossed over into a village. It looks elegant and warm, and I notice the chimneys spouting black smoke. I entered the village and went to the first building to the right.

The outer structure of the building is made up of large tree logs and a mix of stones. It is impossible to see within without peeking through the small window at the top of the door.

As I entered through a large, heavily used wooden door, warm air and an aroma of food and wine. The BarMaid is cleaning while the cook is fast asleep on a chair. The inside is a match to the outside. Large wooden beams support the interior roof, and a row of small, molten candles are attached. The walls are barren. The tavern itself is vacant, except for the BarMaid and Cook.

"Welcome. What can I get for you?" greeted the BarMaid. Who does she think she is speaking to? Her smile and bright eyes bore into me. Oh, right, she doesn't know who I am.

Her blonde hair covers the right side of her face, showing only one green eye. The simple brown dress barely covered her shoulders. A drooping neckline reveals the tops of her pale breasts. I admire her bountiful bosom, and my cock stirs.

"I am looking for a warm place to stay and a nice roast," I answer while rubbing my freezing hands together. Her eyes trail me from head to toe, and my cock decides it needs warming too.

"You aren't from here, are you?" asked the Barmaid. I see a glint of curiosity in her eyes and don't want to raise suspicion.

"No, milady, I am headed towards Orion Fortress to visit my cousin." It's a lie, but it will ensure security for the night.

"I figured only a fool would walk outside in the snow without a cloak." I've heard of snow before, but only in different stories. The scholars made it sound enjoyable, but I disagree wholeheartedly. You can keep your snow.

The BarMaid sets a plate of roast and a glass of wine in front of me, and I salivate at the sight before me. A plump hog leg is set at the center of the plate, with a circle of roasted potatoes and a glass of plum wine. The first bite welcomed a juicy, tender, smoked flavor of ham. The potatoes gave off an earthy flavor that needed to be washed down with a sweet swig of plum wine.

"My name is Katrina, and if there is anything else I can get you…"Her hand caresses my arm, her eyes burning.

"I require a warm place for the night," I answer, the words coming out more husky than expected.

"You can stay here. We have a guest bed and nice fire all night."She gestures toward a closed door opposite the back one.

She grabbed my hand without delay, and we walked quickly towards the room. The door shuts, turning the lock, and our bodies collide. We tear our clothes off each other. I cup her wet pussy. It's not tight, but no whore ever has a fresh cunt. My cock doesn't judge as her fingers grip me, working me until a bead of my seed coats the tip. I push her to her knees, forcing my cock into her hot mouth. She tries to take control, but I don't have time for that. I hit the back of her throat and ram her hard. She gags; her face coated in tears, and her mouth is drooling, but she holds on.

I feel her finger cinching close to my taunt, and I pull out before she can reach it. With a firm grasp on her hair, I force her up, turning her around. Wetting my fingers with her arousal, I pump into her pussy a few times before jamming them into her ass. She screams, her neck craning and back arching.

"I only fuck whores in the ass," I growl in her ear. "Is that okay with you?"

"Yes," she whimpers, pushing backward in response.

"Then you will take my cock. Spread your legs and

bend over."

She obeys, my fingers punishing her taint until I know she is ready. I spit on my hand a couple of times, preparing myself for entry, and then I slam into her. Not giving a fuck about anything but my release.

"Fuck," I scream. She makes a sound and I grab the bed sheet and stuff it into her mouth before I fuck her ass until I'm ready to cum. She reaches for her cunt, just like they all try to do. Get pleasure, but I'm a bastard when it comes to fucking. I will never give a woman pleasure until that woman is mine. Once I claim her, then she'll know what true pleasure is.

I smack her hand away and pull out, then slam back in, and then pull out, finishing myself on her back. I fall back into a chair, my chest rising and falling. "Get a bucket and cloth for us to clean up. Please."

Her knees shake as she stands, and I prepare for hate, but it's feral when she looks at me. "You had your fun," she begins, the sheet in her hand. "Now, it's my turn."

She straddles my limp cock, rubbing her folds on me, and bile rises in my throat. I grip her shoulders, stopping her, and she tries to kiss me; I turn away.

"You'll fuck me in my ass and mouth, but you won't kiss me or give me pleasure?" she asks.

"You want to pleasure yourself; do it in your chambers. I have a long journey, and I need rest." I lift her off me and move over to the bed, pulling another sheet off and cleaning myself. The door slams, and I peek over my shoulder to find only my clothes on the floor. I flop onto my bed, naked and somewhat sedated.

I'm a bastard.

My eyelids closed, and I soon drifted off to sleep.

There is darkness like usual, but then a faint figure of a woman appears before me.

Brown hair flowing in the wind, dark blue eyes, and painted red lips. She wears a silk blue dress covering her breasts but revealing her bare shoulders. The puffed, shortened sleeves stop at the edge of her elbows. The gown is lightweight, comfortable, and fits her figure.

****

Kaleigh

My nails hurt from the persistent picking over the last five minutes of my confession to my sister. She hasn't said a word or made a move to strike me for sounding delusional. Not even when I told her about the sex with Tristian. Her face is stoic, her shoulders tense, and I fight the urge to pace.

When she finally sighs, I slump into the saffron chair next to the flickering warmth of the stones. "I don't know what you want me to say," she whispers, her eyes never meeting mine.

"I feel that the kings of our past sent me those visions as an omen. The man was looking for me. As the heir, perhaps he is an assassin," I suggest.

"Where would he have come from? The barrier separates us from Zoldir and the rest of the world. Not to mention that any man trying to cross blades with you will meet their end. As far as the other part,"—she stands, walks toward the mantle, and stops—"You fucked a servant. Not once, but four times. Have you lost your mind?"

"No, but the barbaric ideology that we have to save our maidenhood until we're married is, well, ridiculous," I snap. She faces me, and where I expect to see anger, I see a smile before the laughter. My resolve falters, and soon I'm clutching my side beside her.

"What are we going to do?" she asks after we contain ourselves. I put my hands on her shoulders and embrace her for appreciation and strength. We break apart, my touch remaining while I look into her eyes and speak my mind.

"We need to stop him. Find this person before he locates me." I wait for her to interject, then drop my hands, creating a small gap between us. "The journey through the forest will be difficult since I've never been. I don't know any trails. But that won't be the most difficult part. It's freezing temperatures."

"I see. Will your lover be there to keep you warm?" she quips.

"I don't believe I should involve him. I'm going to tell him what we have is strictly professional. I mentioned that we are nothing more than friends, but we were interrupted before I could hear if he accepted that."

"Then you should get some rest." Her dismissive tone cuts me, but I don't argue, taking my leave of her.

Departing Abby's room, the small glowing lanterns attached to the varying columns help to light the darkened hall. A few meters away from her chambers are mine. I've always hated the purple doors. The fire was going on when I walked in. A few heated pots of thyme and lilac mask the scent of burning wood.

After a long day like today, I suspect my bath is prepared.

"Just as I like it." I look at the steaming basin filled with water and petals from the garden. I reach for the small table beside my bath; a glass of red wine is prepared for consumption. After several sips, I close my eyes to let the heat soothe my aching body.

Amidst the darkness, a man walked toward me.

"Is this a dream?" I look around as the image becomes brighter, and the man walks faster in my direction. I don't cower away. Standing my ground, I ask, "Stop. Who are you?"

He doesn't stop to answer me. I reach for my sword, but it's nowhere to be found. In one swift moment, he paralyzes me in my spot. A scream erupts from my throat, but nothing comes out of it.

My eyes snap open, jolting me out of the basin in a frenzied scramble. As I wipe water from my eyes, a fit of coughing hits me.

What was that?

After catching my breath, drying, dressing, and guzzling another cup of wine, I tuck myself into thick duvet linens. Staring at the canopy above, I try to sleep, but my mind is restless with thoughts of this man.

I hope you're a prepared stranger because once I get my sights on you, Shadow Striker never misses.

Chapter Three

Rowland

The pack and wool cloak on my back I grabbed outside of my room this morning keep me warm. Unfortunately, no gloves or other garments were available to ward off the cold. Katrina was nowhere to be seen when I made my escape. Not that I had any desire to run into her again. She must not have been too upset to provide me with free lodging, meals, and supplies for my journey to meet the foreign king. Unless she was paying me, thinking that I was the whore.

I laugh at the ridiculous notion and scan my surroundings once more.

Trees and snow. Not a clearing in sight for a few feet that will provide for a good campsite. The snow crunches with each step but I don't slow down until I notice a small hill just beyond the road with an opening in the woods.

With swift determination, I press forward but lose my grip on a rock because of the freezing temperatures that have numbed my fingers. A few more feet, and I'm at the top. There is a small clearing with evidence of a previous campfire. Black scorch marks and ash at the center of a circle of rocks.

Bending down, I hold my hand over it to ensure it's

no longer warm, telling me the people vacated it hours ago, if not before dawn. Picking branches from the ground, I form them in a pile, ready to light. Reaching into my sack, I grab flint and tinder to start a small fire.

A sigh escapes my lips as the sparks light the fire, and warmth coats my hands, melting the lingering chill in my bones. "She may have been a whore, but the bitch must have been pleased because there's a fucking hog leg in here." I don't know who I'm talking to, but the words tumble out on their own accord. Every few seconds, I turn the leg counterclockwise. The smell of meat makes my mouth water, reminisce about the first bite back at the tavern.

A branch cracks behind me.

"Ignore it," I command myself as I pull the meat from the fire, blow on it, and prepare to take a bite. Another snap, and I'm on my feet, one hand gripping bone, the other my hilt. Footsteps approach, and a figure appears out of the shadows seconds later.

"Well, brothers, look what we have here." A chestnut-haired man is approaching with a nasty scar across his face, and four others surround me.

Fuck, I just wanted to eat.

Each one is matching like a band of hooligans. A red garment around each of their heads bearing a griffon at the center. Perhaps if I play nice, so will they.

"Good evening," I greet them with my most diplomatic smile.

"You look like a fancy man. The Red Griffin Bandits do not appreciate fancy men in our territory." He gestures towards his brothers. All wore white furred jackets with long sleeves that touched the leather bands around their wrists. Their thick brown trousers, held up by black leather belts, tightened with knots on the right side of their legs. Each wearing knee-high boots stained with blood.

"I assure you, I did not know," I responded. "My name is Rowland, and I'm just eating for the night before I continue on my way to my cousins in Sumter."

He nods, but the look of disbelief on his face is unnerving.

"It seems like we can help you out. My name is Zeke, and I believe that Sumter is to the west, and you're traveling north towards King Dekka's territory. He doesn't do kindly to strangers."

"Thank you for the warning. I'll just finish up and be on my way." I state, bending my knees slightly until I see it from the corner of my right eye. Jerking backward as the tip of a blade crosses right in front of my eyes, missing its intended target and burying itself into a tree.

"Make this easy for yourself. Give us everything on your person, and we will kill you quickly."

"A generous offer." I smirk. The others move in closer. One of them is huge with a mace in his hand. I choose him first and angle myself to attack. "I've got a better idea." Without giving them time, I throw the leg in the eyes of the big one and draw my sword.

"I'm gonna kill you, boy!" he yells.

His veins throb in his head and neck as he wields a steel mace head full of tendrils, swinging it with brute force. The clinking of metal expresses sparks in the air.

My feet slide backward with the resistance he is pushing against me. I kept glancing to my rear, and just as I suspected, one of his brothers charged with his own sword. Leaping back and whirling, their weapons rang in my ears. I take advantage of this new position behind him, kicking his knees forward forcing him to fall on top of his smaller sibling.

I turn to flee but am met with a snickering, bald-looking man wielding two blackened blades curved into a crescent point. I parry the first strike but not fast enough to avoid a piercing cut to my cheek.

Lunging forward, slashing, I give him a gash to match mine along his forearm. He wails in pain. The force I used was just enough to slice through the skin down to the bone just below the elbow. Blood squirting out all over the ground turns the beautiful snow a dark red. The injured man falls to the ground, screaming, holding his hand over his wound.

"Dew, stop moving." The big guy races over to help him. After ensuring there are no more attackers, I turn and run. I don't make it very far because a wall of two bodies tackles me into the ground. My vision is blurred as my skull connects with something hard.

When I get control of my footing, I scramble to my feet and stare at two identical twins. "How many more of you are there?" My words are breathless, and my throat is burning. They smile, and I take a step backward, looking past them at the others. The oldest one who challenged me was standing there barking at the big one and injuring another one.

This is my chance to flee.

I look towards the ground and notice a clump of frost-covered dirt.

Perfect.

I fall to my knees, feigning surrender. "I give up. Please."

They laugh and approach. When the one on the left

closes the distance, I grab the rock, swinging with all my strength, and crack it against his head. Knocking him to the ground, unconscious and bleeding. I don't wait to admire my work. Picking up my sword, I run.

****

Kaleigh

Today will be the start of a new adventure. It's what I tell myself every morning when my reflection is staring back at me through the looking glass. I braided my hair in two separate tails; managing this way is easier. I put on the winter clothes Roselina had made for me last year when a cold storm came in from the snow forest.

"You're awake?" Roselina's question comes as she enters with my breakfast tray.

"Yes, I can dress myself." I smile at her.

"Going on a hunt? Would you like your food wrapped?" She asks.

"Yes." It's better to keep a routine so she doesn't suspect anything.

"Is there another cold storm? Shall I gather more wood from the carver?" She begins to exit, and I think of an excuse.

"No. I just want to wear this today." I smile. "It's beautiful and deserves to be shown about."

Not sure if she believes me, I don't waste another minute before making a swift exit. She'll stick with her chores and make no more fuss over me and my wardrobe choices. The smell of roasted duck makes my mouth water as I enter the kitchen. The chef, whose real name is Rodney, is busy at work.

"Good morning, Princess."

"Good morning, Chef. Can I get some quail eggs,

roasted duck, bread, and a goblet of milk, please?" Wearing a blue blouse, black trousers, and a white apron tied in the back, he bows and prepares my food. It's the one thing I truly love about the man. No questions asked; just do what he is told. Or so I thought.

"That sounds like a hearty breakfast. Going on a hunt later?" Chef inquired.

"You could say that." I smile. Why is everyone so interested in my hunts today?

Wandering into the pantry, four shelves are full of different ingredients. Going to the pantry shelf, I grab fresh bread, head back into the kitchen, and fill my waterskin.

"Here you go, Your Highness. Bring me back some horn rabbits, and I'll make your favorite stew." He smiles and then turns back to work.

With my food portions packed, next is weapons.

I make my way toward the armory, and it's only a few right turns and a leftover. The hairs on the back of my neck rise and the sound of distant footsteps has me on edge. Someone is following me. I step behind one pillar. A few heartbeats later, my sister's shadow passes me, of course.

"Abby, why are you following me?" I challenge her before stepping out of the shadows behind her.

She stopped and turned to face me before saying, "I should have known I couldn't hide from you."

"You think."

"Ever since our conversation last night, I couldn't help but think that you would find that mystery man." She shrugs her shoulders, looking down at her feet.

"Maybe I am, or maybe I am just going on a long hunting trip."

"You can't fool me, sis. I want to help." She smiles. A little too eagerly.

"All right, I only packed enough extra food for three days," I told her.

Abbygale takes her bag off her back, opens it, and shows me her food. "It's okay, I brought my own. If you do not let me come with you, I will tell Mother."

"Abby, you're twenty-three. I thought we were past the age of immaturity?" I cock a brow, and she crosses her arms in a challenge. Tossing my hands up, I figure out what I have to lose. "All right, fine, but I don't want to hear any complaining."

Making our way into the armory, an arched stone doorway with a profoundly used steel door was open. Once inside, there are shelves lined with armor and various weapons, and the smell of musk lingers in the air.

"Oh, your Highnesses. Good morning. How may I be of service to you today?" Tristian is covered in black ink and smells of metal. Clearing is tasked with polishing the guard's armor.

"Good morning, Tristian. I am taking Abby out on her first hunt." I avoid making eye contact with him but notice Abby staring at him. She knows our secret. I could slap myself for trusting her not to tease us.

"How exciting." Sensing a slight tone of anger in his voice, I narrow my eyes at him in warning.

"I need two sets of quivers, a few dozen arrows, two hunting knives, and two swords." Stopping what he was doing, bewilderment came across his face.

"Umm, forgive me, but that is a lot of weaponry for one hunting trip."

"Do what you are told, peasant." Abby deemed.

"Abby, there is no need to be rude," I state, trying to avoid any conflict.

"Sorry, please do not question us," Abby recanted in a sarcastic tone.

He looks at me, tilting his head toward a spot on the other side of the room. It's a signal that he wants to speak in private. I don't have time for this. Fuck! I scream internally.

"Sister, pick out something while I speak to Tristian," I command, and she cuts her eyes at me but begins admiring the wall of daggers.

"Has your sister ever held a weapon?" he whispers as we make our way out of earshot.

"Does it matter? She's my blood. I'm sure there's a warrior in that bodice of hers just aching to be released."

He smiles. "That's what I love about you." He reaches for me, but I step back. "I'm in love with you, Kaleigh, and I know you're lying to me. Tell me the truth about why you're here."

"Tristian, I need to make this very clear. You're my friend, and nothing can ever come of this. You have no right to question why I need weapons because you're just a servant, and I'm the princess and heir to the throne." There, I said it. Plain as day.

"Fine. One of these days, you'll see no one better for you than me." He then taps my nose. I slap his hand away and then proceed to grab my weapons.

Making our way to the stables, each of the ten cubbies housing one horse, only divided by a single wall. My horse, an Orion Walker named Ivy, has a black bodice with a white mane and gentle black eyes. Opposite Abby's, Stella has white fur, with a black mane.

We saddle our horses, and despite what everyone else might think about my baby sister, she's a quick study and knows much more than she leads on. We wouldn't get along so well if she didn't.

"It will be cold in the Snow Forest. We must buy some wool coats and supplies for a fire."

"We will need to go to the market for that." Once mounted, we trot over the bridge and into the marketplace. Approaching a vendor while Abby stayed a few feet away with the horses, I was greeted with a warm welcome.

"Welcome, Your Highness; what can I get you today?"

"I need supplies." I placed two coats, granitic and kindling, on the tabletop.

"Going on a hunt, are we?" the shopkeeper asks while gazing at my bundle of weapons atop her horse.

"Something like that." I keep it short and to the point. I've got to stop being so obvious. It's a good thing no one has ever suspected what Tristian and I are up to in the woods.

After paying for the supplies, I pack them onto the horse, dividing them evenly before marching toward the border into the forbidden forest. There is little light and no green in sight. I look at my sister. "Are you sure about this?"

"You'll need someone you can trust in there. Who is better than me?" She smiles, and then shows me two daggers strapped to either thigh.

"Hey, wait for me!" We snap our attention behind us, and then I see him.

"Tristan?" Abby questions. "What the fuck are you

doing here?"

"You don't think you are leaving without me, do you?" he struggled to say while catching his breath.

"You were supposed to stay behind. And where is your horse?" My sister interrogates me, and I let her because what I want to say to him is far worse.

"I can't let my best friend go on a dangerous mission without me. I didn't want to raise suspicion."

"So, you ran? How smart is that?" Abby questioned.

"I suppose not. You can ride with Abby since I have most of the supplies on my horse." Abby shot me a look of discouragement, but I ignored it.

Taking the lead, I pull my cloak tight around me and kick Ivy into a small trot across the border.

Chapter Four

Rowland

Fuck those bandits!

It's freezing, my clothes are wet, and my stomach groans in pain. I've been out here for hours. The snowfall covered my tracks and ruined my chance of returning to the path. Above, I see what looks like an opening to a cave. My legs are burning with each impact of the climb. Curse this blasted place. When I finally reach the top, I give myself a moment of reprieve to catch my breath. Useless and painful, but I walk inside a dark area covered in snow and animal bones.

Leaning against the interior stone wall, I collapse onto the ground, placing my head between my knees, and thanking the great kings to be shielded from the biting wind. Exhaustion attempts to overtake me, but I stagger to my feet and look for a spot to clear for a fire.

"I'll have to make one," I grumble when I see none. The White Sun is high, and the lip of the cave doesn't allow enough of the beam to seep through to make it easier to see. With numb, cracked, and shaking hands, I scoop a thin layer of snow from the bottom until I see the stone. As I walk out to find some bramble, I pull my cloak tighter around me, appreciating I didn't lose it during the fight. I find a few good ones and return inside, knocking two stones together to create a spark. When it failed to catch, I unsheathed my sword and cut the bottom of my cloak. It's thick, and only the bottom seam is wet.

I run it along the sharpened edge a few times until it frays. Placing it at the pile's center, I work on igniting it again.

"Thank the kings!"The flames catch. Laying down, staring at the roof of the cave, my stomach twists in pain, but I'm too exhausted to look for food. Warmth and sleep are a priority at the moment.

Standing in a foreign room, I am face to face with a woman dressed in a silk nightgown. The most beautiful woman I've ever laid my eyes on. She was close enough for me to touch her. Without thinking about it, I run my fingers along her soft cheek. "Who are you?"

"Rowland, I am yours, and you're mine. When we meet, a test will be completed for the hearts of stones are depleted," she answered as she faded into the shadows. I miss her touch almost immediately and begin to chase her into the darkness.

I snap awake, sitting up with a wince and looking around. The enclosed space reminds me of where I am and what occurred these past two days. Something knocks against the toes of my boots.

Fuck!

Gripping my sword, I slowly release it from its sleeve, watching as a giant polar beast sniffs my heels.

When my sword is nearly free, its black eyes meet mine, and I know I'm screwed. Rolling to my side, I ignore the pain. Surviving a bear attack is highly unlikely, but if I can kill it—that's enough food for a month, maybe two. Springing to my feet, stumbling, I face the predator, and it growls. The massive beast has large teeth designed for shredding bone, and stained with blood from its last kill. There were scars in place of missing patches of fur, and his stone-cold black eyes glared at me with anger and hunger.

"Come on, then!" Yelling at the beast isn't the smartest thing I've ever done, but if I am to die, at least I will go down fighting. Charging at me with a large swiping paw, I jumped out of the way and stabbed the bear in the side. The beast scowled and growled with anger. It turned to swipe at me again. I was quick but not enough to avoid a sharp, slicing pain across my back. A mixture of fire and ice coats my back, and I can smell iron. There is no time to check for wounds as I see an opening and run for the exit.

Climbing onto the ledge at the entrance, I waited for an opportune moment. As suspected, it follows me, and I jump, straddling the beast's neck. I grip its scruff to maintain balance, but its large body weight is thrashing me back and forth. I cry out in pain as my back connects with the wall, and I nearly fall over.

With one hand dead gripping his neck, the other on my hilt, I angle it toward the center of his neck and thrust it downward with all the strength I have left. The beast makes several noises before falling to the floor with a loud thud. I lay on top of it, listening to its slow heart. When his final breath escapes him, and the thrumming stops, I close my eyes briefly.

I awake hours later as the High Sun's rays seep through the entrance, noting a new day. Grimacing in pain, I sit up and reach around, my fingers touching something wet. Blood. "That'll need mending." My muscles groaned having slept on top of the bear. I half-slide, half-fall off its back, my knees and palms bracing the impact of the ground. I catch a handful of snow and press it onto my wounds to numb them. "Damn, that hurts."

It's a burning sensation at first, but soon the pain fades, and I slice a long, rectangular piece of wool around my torso to cover the wounds.

Great kings of the past, why a bear? Why couldn't it have been a rabbit? Bastards.

I've never been this close to death before, and now I have three large holes in my wool cloak. I look at the dead animal and crawl over to it. Allowing the fur to cover me in warmth. My thoughts drifted to Father and the first hunting lesson he gave me and Gregor. "When you kill an animal, you must honor the sacrifice by making use of the many blessings it will bring."

The wound would have to wait, and I would have to work through this pain. It took me the rest of the day to skin the bear, fighting through exhaustion. When I decided to rest, I packed snow along the beast to help keep it preserved. Reigniting the fire, it went out during the morning. I cupped a handful of snow and placed both over the heat of the flames. It quickly melts, and I drink it.

"A few more minutes, and then it will be time to finish. Thank the kings, you're a small thing but large enough to feed me." Knowing the smell of the meat might attract some unwanted company, I look for animal scars and collect them. Once I have enough, I rub it around the entrance and leave smaller piles on the floor. Over the course of a few days, I worked on the beast. Melting snow into water, cutting slices of meat for cooking. By the time I was done, my wounds scabbed over, and half the carcass was gone. There isn't a point in me staying here any longer. That night, cuddled under the fur coat, I spoke out loud. I don't know if it helps, but I have to believe someone is listening. "Tomorrow, I'll journey out. Find that village and forget about this perilous mission. Maybe find myself buried in a willing whore with a tankard of ale and belly of roast."

****

The next day, I left my cave, using the High Sun as guidance to journey north, knowing it rises west. There is no snowfall, which is a blessing. I try to keep my body in the rays of the High Sun to add warmth, although the cloak and fur are fine. I'm not sure I'll ever take home for granted again. A couple of hours into the journey, my body screams for a break. The tops of the trees provided shade, the small beams of light from the High Sun glistened off the snow, and the quietness of the area was tranquil. I set up a small fire, using the beast's skull and skin to contain the smoke. Wouldn't want to have a run-in with those bandits or, worse, another beast.

It also gave a smoky flavor to the bear meat, which fluttered my stomach in delight.

After eating, I checked my wounds, touching them. "Not bleeding, warm to the touch, and no liquid. That's good." I felt a dull pain, numbed by the snow, I pressed on it. When it was time to move on, I repacked everything, smothered the fire with snow and dirt from nearby, grabbed my supplies, and headed north again.

A rushing sound that reminded me of a spring caught my ears in the far-off distance. I halted and listened. It was in the opposite direction of the High

Sun.

Rushing water means a stream, and a stream could lead to a larger body of water or even a village. Painfully, I tried to run toward the sound, but it was a hobble at best. When I finally came across a creek, I followed the flow, drawing my sword in case I ran into any more predators. Approaching the end of the beginning of the flow, I stopped when I saw a narrow brook glistening in the light as it ran off the top of a frosted mountain into a pool of water.

A waterfall and a mountain to climb. Of course, the bastards in the sky couldn't make it a simple staircase. Cursing the kings and gods won't help me get up the mountain faster. The journey up the side of the mountain was slippery, uneven, and more difficult than expected. Each grip of a stone was met with resistance.

A loud noise sounded all around, and a large shadow glided across the mountainside.

Please don't be another fucking bear.

I pull myself onto a small ledge, using the fur to help camouflage me in the snow. I scan the path behind me for the owner of the shadow but see nothing. Then I hear it again. The sound mocking a bird's wings. Looking toward the skies, I see it but can't believe it to be true.

This is not possible. My eyes must deceive me. Ice Dragons used to be the guardians of all royals that could travel anywhere. The High Council and Grand Council of the Old Worlds killed the dragons after one of them betrayed their master.

I watched and waited for its next move. It flew through the waterfall and into the mouth of the cave. "Don't be a fool. Just keep moving. An ancient beast will eat us. There is nothing remotely interesting about a dragon." My feet move on their own accord, and soon, I find myself back at the bottom, staring at the waterfall. "Fuck. Since I'm down here, I might as well be sure I saw what I saw."

There was a sliver of an opening between water and stone. I squeezed through, firmly pressed to the wall, and looked inside. I couldn't see past my hand, but I didn't need to. A presence was there. I could feel the warmth of its breath, feel the vibrations with each step it took. Then I saw it. Two sparkling blue eyes, as big as my head, looking directly at me. Its mouth opened, and I prepared myself to meet the god of death.

"Welcome, My Lord."

Chapter Five

Kaleigh

Snow rains upon us, keeping the reserve of warmth nearly impossible. Abby and Tristian huddled close, the protest from before gone as the instinct of survival takes over. Scanning the area ahead, I spot a nice clearing to make camp for the night. The thick bramble and circle of trees will help protect us against the night wind. Stopping, I slide from my saddle to go to the spot. Removing a glove, I feel the ground is dry enough to make a small fire.

"We'll camp here for the evening. Tie the horses off around the circle. Their bodies will help keep us warm," I tell them.

"How far until we make it to the village?" Abby asks. I suspected a tone of regret, but she appeared to be enjoying her time away from the solitude of the castle.

"Unfortunately, the Ice Village is not for another fifty miles. So, we must camp before the High Sun turns to white." I grip Ivy's reins and walk her over to the tree, securing her to it before unpacking her saddle.

My traveling companions are silent as they continue to work. Tristian steals glances at me, winking every three seconds and nodding toward the trees. He wants to have sex out here. What is wrong with him?

"I will go over here. I think I see some dry leaves

just beyond those trees." Tristian announces. I look at Abby, who, just like me, ignores his innuendo.

When he disappears behind the brush, I approach my sister. "How long should we leave him alone for?" she asks.

"Let him freeze his cock off. The bastard clearly doesn't understand what the term friends means."

"You shouldn't have started it. A man like him with a woman like you, he was surely to hold on tight." It didn't sound like an insult to my intelligence, but it still stung like one.

"I will gather the food," I whisper, walking away to take out the provisions. Once the stack was ready, I struck the flint and tinder, smiling once the flames formed within the circle of stones. While finishing setting up the tent, I noticed a missing member of the team "Where is Tristian?"

"He probably got his cock stuck where it doesn't belong," Abby muses. When I don't laugh, she sighs and says, "I haven't seen him since he left." I go in the direction he went, my instincts telling me something is off. I pick up his trail in the snow, following it for a few feet until stumbling upon a trail of blood. Bending down, I touch it, noticing its warmth.

"Tristian?" Fearing a wolf or bear attacked him, I call out again, "Tristian!" The sound of cracking branches and thundering footfalls has me drawing my sword. Out of the bushes comes my sister, her hands raised. "I heard you calling out. You haven't found him?"

I shook my head. "No, but I found fresh blood. Wherever he is, he's injured."

Abby looks ahead, gesturing her hand for me to

take the lead. A silent move of support, words unnecessary because we both know that leaving the man to die isn't right.

The further we travel, the deeper into the forest we move, and I fear we may lose sight on the way back. Red droplets soon develop into long drag marks across the ground, painting the fresh powder with blood.

"Do I need to say it?"I don't acknowledge her. "All right, since you won't say it. By the looks of the blood, he's either dead or mostly dead. And whatever it is, it's strong enough to take him down and drag him twenty feet away from the campsite."

I continue to ignore her, part of me not wanting to entertain the idea that one of my only friends might be dead, and the other part. I just don't want to go there mentally.

Distant voices and the glow of burning woods stop me in my tracks. I squint to get a better visual but see nothing but the tips of flickers and the rise of smoke swirls.

We move closer, getting on our hands and knees to match the height of the bushes and keep our presence hidden. "I don't think it was a beast that took your lover," Abby whispers, her widened eyes mortified at the sight before us. The center of the clearing is an enormous bonfire. Five men surround it. Two appear to be recently injured. Their green bandages bear the mark of a skilled healer. A rose is a symbol of bandages with magical properties.

Tristan is tied to a tree trunk, his eyes closed and head slanted to one side. I can't see where the blood is coming from. "We need to get into that big tent. I bet it's the leader's, by the looks of it." A tan triangular tent held up by wooden logs is at the far end of the camp. There is a red griffin painted over the front entrance. "I want to see who we are dealing with before we attempt a rescue."

My sister appears to be paralyzed with fear by the looks of her erect posture.

"Abby." I cup her cold cheeks, forcing her gaze to mine. "Are you with me?"

"I'm not a trained fighter, Sis." She's scared, and it's my job to reassure her. "You know enough. What about those daggers? I know you've been practicing with them."

"For a month, only after that cat got into my bedroom and tried to bite me." She's on the defensive. Her lip is quivering, teeth are shaking. I wrap my arms tightly around her, giving her some of my strength.

"I need your back on this one. Once we know who these men are, I promise you we will save Tristian and never have to see them again." I don't like making risky reassurance, but I believe this one is warranted.

"Okay," she whispers.

Making our way around the outside of the bramble, I find the perfect spot to get through undetected. There are no guards on the backside of the tent. Gripping one of Abby's daggers, I slice a gap just enough for us to crawl through. Keeping the dagger in hand, I go in first. With it vacant, I hear Abby's sighs of relief, and we begin scrummaging around. There isn't much inside the space. A tethered black rug covers the bottom of the tent with a bed lined with the fur of an elk and a hawk feather pillow. Perpendicular is a wooden desk covered in parchments and blood-stained coin purses. The smell of musk and alcohol has my stomach churning.

"Kaleigh, I think these are the Red Griffin Bandits," Abby exclaims, examining the parchments on the desk. "These are traveling routes for the palace treasures." Grabbing them from her, I scoff in disbelief but then vaguely remember Father mentioning something about a robbery.

"I remember Father telling me about them once before. They are a ruthless bunch of criminals. Father has had the royal guard after them for years," Abbygale explains. She was always better at politics than I was.

"Who the hell are you?" I swing around, coming face to face with a man pointing his blade directly at Abbygale's throat. "You are a pretty little thing, aren't you? Maybe we should get better acquainted." Tears roll down my sister's cheeks, while fury unleashes inside of me. His fingers trail down her neck, cupping her breast, and I step forward. "Any closer, and I slit her from chin to navel."

"Let my sister go, and I promise no harm will come to you," I negotiate, knowing it is useless with men like him.

"You have the nerve to come into my home and threaten me?" He laughs, his tongue darting out to lick her. Bile rises in my throat, but I swallow it down. I look at Abby, nodding to show her she will come out of this. She blinks once in response. I watch as her left-hand inches toward her other dagger.

Distract him. "I'm sorry for the intrusion. Take me in place of my sister."

His eyes gleam triumphantly, and he points his blade at me while keeping a loose hold on my sister. "Strip."

I raise my hands to the claps on my cloak, giving

43

my sister the necessary diversion. In a blur of blades and blood, Abby bucked, pulling her blade free before thrusting it into the man's gut. She cups her hands to her face, horrified, as she backs into my arms.

"It's okay. You had to," I whisper against her hair. He pulls the blade free, blood running out of the sides of his mouth before he falls forward, the god of death reaping his soul. Giving Abby a moment to console herself, I clean the blade, and taking his, I turn to her. "Take it back. I have a plan, but I need Shadow Striker."

With shaky hands, she grabs it and places it back in its sleeve. I grip her hand, pulling her out of the back and into the dark forest again.

****

With my bow and quiver of arrows, I move and make my way back to the spot where I left Abby. "Easy, it's just me," I say when she turns around, ready to stab me.

"They haven't found his body yet," she whispers. Nothing I can do or say to her will help her heal. My goal is to get us all out of this alive. "Just tell me what you need me to do." She looks at me and my heart shatters at the sight of her unrecognizable defeat.

"Crawl through the bushes until you get to the tree he's tied to. From the position they are standing at, it will be difficult for them to spot you behind it. I need you to cut him down. I will be in this tree watching over you. Once you're both in the clear, I want you to run. Go back home, and don't turn back."

"You want me to leave you?" she asks with an incredulous look on her face.

"It was a mistake for me to think we can do this

with just the three of us. I want you and Tristian safe before I can devise another plan. I will be right behind you." I press her forehead to my lips, whispering, "I promise."

We broke apart, both getting into position. I watch over her like I said, ensuring she makes it to him safely. When the cutting begins, I loosely knock an arrow, ensuring not strain myself.

One man turns to face Tristian. He looks inquisitively at him, and I pull back, sighting in on my target. He turned back around, and I breathed, relaxing my bow again. I keep my eyes trained on the scene, and when she gives me the signaling whistle from our childhood, I knock my arrow. Aiming it at the far end where they keep their cooking pots. I release it on a breath and climb down, not waiting to see if I hit.

The chorus of voices picks up, and I peek over the bushes to watch as the men run in the opposite direction of my sister and friend. I catch up to them. Abby is struggling to keep Tristian on his feet. I grab his other arm, adding my strength, and we take off. "I knew you would find me." His voice faltered, and I saw his lips were blue and cracked. "Take my cloak. I will support you, but you must stay quiet." Wrapping Tristian in the wool, I shiver at the gust of wind. He needs it more than I do. A shout of alarm comes from the encampment, and then the pounding of feet follows in our direction. I push them behind the trunk of a large oak tree.

"Stay here. I'll distract them. Remember what I told you." I don't wait for them to protest as I take off on foot. "Hey, come and get me!"

"Get them!"

Running through various trees, making little knick

marks as I go, I wait until I am far away before climbing another tree. Once in the crook of the branches, I knock my arrow once more and aim.

"Where are they?" I watch in horror as the man Abby stabbed comes striding in at the head of the pack. His hand was on his wound. "You were supposed to be watching that boy!" He attempts to hit one of them.

A yell of protest comes from another, and just as I didn't see it coming, neither did he. The leader's head falls to the snow, body collapsing in an increasing pool of red.

"Let's get out of here." The men run off in the opposite direction.

"That was an unexpected turn of events," I whisper to myself.

I wait for a few more minutes before making my way back to solid ground. Once my feet hit the ground, I ran. I found some of my nicks, but then I didn't. "Where is it? Where the fuck is it?"

My lungs are on fire, and my chest feels like it's caving with the increased rate of my heart.

I run and run until my knees impact the snow. My body is numb, vision is blurring until I see something through the beams of the White Sun. At the top of a small hill is the mouth of a cave. There is animal scat, bones, and a leftover carcass. I ignore it all, slumping against the inner wall, grateful for the windbreak.

I spot the remains of a fire and find the will to gather the leftover animal bits to build a small fire. With the sharpened tip of my arrow, I knock it against a stone until sparks ignite and warmth fills the cave.

Darkness begins to cloud my vision, and slumber beckons me.

I find myself standing in the middle of the forest, face to face with the man from before. I draw my sword against him and swing. His blade connects with mine. He's quick to move. Our blades disappear, and his grip is on my wrist, pulling me into him. I tried to speak, but again, nothing came out. He smirked, his dark eyes glinting with something I'd never seen before.

"You are my destiny, Kaleigh, and I am yours." He leans forward, his lips caressing my cheek, sending waves of heat through me. "Stay on the path, and you will be reunited with me soon."

Chapter Six

Rowland

"There is no need for you to be afraid," the dragon states, its wide mouth not reassuring me. "Let me shed some light for you to see." The cave was lit with blue fire, bringing the beast into perfect view. Sharp blue eyes sit gracefully within the creature's smooth, narrow skull, which gives the dragon a peaceful-looking appearance. Two large brown horns sit symmetrically atop its head, and abreast are two cat-like ears. Its nose had two curved nostrils.

A muscular neck runs down from its head and into a massive body. The skin is covered in perfectly white scales, and small horns run down its spine. Four huge limbs carry the weight of such a magnificent creature. Each claw has four digits. Each nail is sharpened to a point. Its graceful wings were tucked into its shoulders, but from what I could tell, they were massive. Its elegant tail ends with one horn and is covered in the same white scales that match the rest of the body.

"How is this real? How can I hear you speak?" This is an illusion brought on by my current state of mind. It's a perfect explanation for something as incredulous as a talking beast. A dragon in particular.

"Only those of royal blood can, unless I deem a person worthy," it simply states as if that is common knowledge. If I can recall my schooling, there must have been a mention. Or at least in one of the books I read about dragons.

My knees quake, my hands tremble, my vision spots as I fall to the ground.

"You're injured." Its large head moves close to me. I tell my body to move, but the blood loss has me too weak.

"I am fine." It comes out weak.

"I smell the blood." Opening her mouth, I attempt to lift my sword, giving the last of my strength to fight, but it falls from my grip. Heat spreads throughout my body, erasing the pain. I can feel my strength returning to me as I sit up.

"You've healed me. Why?" I stumble to my feet, picking my sword up as I straighten.

"You're Rowland Kawthorne, Lord of Zoldir and future realm king. You're destined to break the curse that has fouled our world for centuries." Her blue eyes glint in admiration as she explains her reasons. "My name is Verglas. I'm one of the last Ice Dragons on this earth."

"Verglas." The Ice Dragon's name was as beautiful as she was. "So, the stories are true?"

"Unfortunately, yes, the past kings of the old world have hunted, captured, and drained to kill my kin."

"Drained to kill? What do you mean? I was told your kind betrayed and killed one of its masters."

"Lies!" Verglas snarled. I leap backward, surprised by her fierceness I wasn't expecting.

I bow my head to her and sheathe my sword to show I'm willing to trust her. "I meant no offense. I wish to learn the truth from your side. This is a rarity that even the books could not provide me."

"After the Dragon Wars ended, King Arnold Orion had a heart full of vengeance. He used his resources to drain our own." She paused, remembering. "King Richard Kawthorne, your greatest grandfather and first king, tried to stop the genocide of my kind. He was met with betrayal and exiled to the world on the other side of the barrier."

"How did our kind get created?"

"Others who learned of the cruel kings' deeds were left alone. I knew you were a descendant of the generous king by the smell of your blood and the prophecy of our meeting. Which, to answer your earlier question, is why I healed you."

"Thank you, Verglas. I do not know how to repay you." She nods appreciatively. We continued talking about how I came to be here until I fell into a deep sleep. The warmth of the cave and the feeling of safety coaxed me into the abyss.

She appeared again, just as before, just as beautiful. With her hand pressed against my chest, she says. "Destiny awaits us."

"What do you mean? Where can I find you?"

"Where the cold ends and summer begins, we will be united when the journey ends."

****

Snapping awake, I scan my surroundings, trying to figure out if last night was all a dream. When my eyes land on the sleeping dragon, it all clicks.

What a magnificent creature. If only Gregor could see me now. Talking with a dragon. Stirring awake, Verglas blinks and lets out a giant yawn before asking, "Having trouble sleeping, are we?"

"No," I state, not wanting to tell her about these troubling dreams.

"I heard you stirring in your sleep."

Standing to stretch, I recant my last thought, thinking about the consequences of telling her about my troubles. When I conclude that there could be none, I answer honestly. "The same dream happens night after night."

"Some dreams are powerful enough to be prophecies or visions," Verglas states while nuzzling a clutch of eggs I don't recall seeing last night. "Tell me about them. I will see if I can help."

"What would be the point? They're mere fantasies. I have no power. I'm no warlock." She swings her snout toward me, a brow raised in curiosity. I can see she will not let up on this from her burning eyes. "It starts with darkness. A woman approaches me in a beautiful blue-gray gown made of silk. She touches me and says I am her destiny."

Something of a hum leaves her throat as she leans closer to assess me. She reaches out with a talon, touching my forehead and my heart. I don't move for fear of consequence. A few breaths pass, and she speaks. "You have the gift of sight."

"Gift of what?" I inquire, unsure if I heard her correctly.

"The gift of sight is a rare and powerful magic. It is a blessing and a curse." Her eyes shrouded in sympathy.

I toss my hands up in exasperation, having never heard something so absurd. "Do you honestly expect me to believe that?"

"You didn't believe in dragons, yet I'm standing

here talking to you." She has a point. "I assure you, it is very real. You must take precautions."

I stayed silent, unsure if anything I could say would add to the conversation. I'll admit my curiosity has peaked. "I didn't start having these dreams until I crossed into this world. Once I get home, will they stop?"

"Perhaps, but when you came into Orion's realm, you awoke the power in yourself and, no doubt, this woman."

"You mean, could she have the same curse? How is that possible?"

She sighs, her scales furrowing above her eyes, making her ears twitch. "This woman, do you know her?"

"No, I have never seen her before." At my response, she makes her way out of the cave, and I duck to avoid getting knocked over by her long, spiked tail, then follow her to the pool of water. I watch as her tongue touches the water; and blue sparks shimmer, illuminating the spot.

"What are you doing?" I ask, but she doesn't answer. My feet begin to move. I try to stop, but I can't. I turn to look away, and I can't snap my eyes from the sight before me.

Fire, death, shadows. War is brewing everywhere, and only the unity of fire and ice can save us.

"Rowland!" A woman screams in pain. "Rowland, where are you?" I look for her through the smoke, but it's too thick.

"Kaleigh!" The name comes to me. I don't know how I know it. Sprinting through the fog of war, I search for her. Calling out her name, my voice croaks, my eyes burn, and I fall to my knees. Something warm against my hands. Looking down, I see blood coating my fingers, a dagger protruding out of a woman's chest before me. I meet her eyes, tears falling down each beautiful pool of ocean. "You were supposed to protect me. Help me save our world from all this, but you betrayed me."

I'm jerked backward, gasping for air, shivering as water drips from my hair. "What the fuck was that?"

"A test," she answers softly; I feel the warmth spread over me, drying all the water from my clothes and skin. "You must go once you are at full strength. Find the woman in your visions and never leave her side again."

"What? Why did you do that? Did I cause that...that war?"

She was silent for a moment before answering. "Prophecies are unpredictable, Rowland. They show you possible outcomes. You and her fail each other in the one you saw, bringing famine to our world. But, there is still time to prevent that from happening."

"Are you telling me I or this Kaleigh might be the harbinger of death?"

"You heard her name? What else has she told you?" The urgency in her tone unnerves me, but I remember everything she said to me last night.

"Where the cold ends and summer begins, we will be united when the journey ends." She groans, "This is worse than I feared."

Why does a dragon terrified of dreams scare me more than that bear? "What is, Verglas? What does she mean by this?"

"A long time ago, two different beings had the

same gift as you. One used it for good and the other for evil. Rowland, there are two paths ahead at the end of your journey. Unity or death." She leans down to meet my eye, those bright blue burning with intensity as she says, "There is nothing more important than you and Kaleigh becoming one. No matter what it takes. No matter what the price is. You can't betray one another, or death will win."

Chapter Seven

Kaleigh

The next day, I awoke with a new determination to make it back home. This mission was foolish from the start. I should have known, basing it on a side effect and dream. Back on the solid ground of the forest, I begin my journey west. Every hunter knows the High Sun rises from the west, and Orion is always at the same point as the sun. With the security of the cave a few hours back, my feet are aching for me to stop, but I can't. It will be mid-sun soon. Stopping will cause a loss of time I can't afford.

A few hours into my trek, I pause briefly to listen for any sign of a fresh spring. After moments pass, I hear nothing. Smacking my lips, it feels like I have cotton lodged in my throat. I swallow painfully but keep moving. A branch cracks under my feet, and the retreating sound of animals rings familiar in my ears. Reaching for my Shadow Striker, I loosely knock an arrow, knowing that any prey would make a good meal at this point.

I pause, inhale, and exhale, raise my bow to position, and wait. My arm begins to tremble, something I'm not used to, but it makes sense because I haven't missed a meal since I was nursing. My eyes divert to the forest floor. When I spot another fallen branch, I stomp on it. Quickly aiming to the skies, I release an arrow, watching as it misses its target.

"Fuck!" I fall to my knees, prickling tears reaching the surfaces of my eyes and stinging my cheeks as O let them tumble. "I've never felt so weak before."

Clearly, I'm losing my mind if talking to an inanimate object is my new normal. Pulling myself together, I stand, forcing one foot in front of the other. When I reach the spot where I shot my arrow, I look for it everywhere but can't locate it. Then I see it. Just beyond the bramble, I'd recognize the fine horse hair of the knock anywhere. The closer I move, the more my vision tunnels until I pull it from the ground. Putting it back in my quiver, I lean forward slightly, something rushing in my ears. I think it's my blood for a second, but I listen closely.

Water.

A stream.

Jumping to my feet, I run. I won't stop until my hands are in the stream, cupping it and running down my throat. It doesn't take long for the freezing temperature to numb my hands. I brush them off, stick them into the inseam of my pants, and lean forward to put my mouth directly in the flow path. It soothes my aching pipe and wets my dry mouth. After a few moments, I sit up and wipe my face on my sleeve. Standing, I follow the flow, praying it will lead to a village water source.

I keep my weary eyes locked on the scenes ahead. When I reach the end, or perhaps the beginning, I halt. Mesmerized by the pure beauty of a clear waterfall.

I don't see the attack coming until I'm knocked off her feet into the pool of water at the base of the falls.

The ice-cold water stabs me with a thousand knives as my lungs constrict. Kicking my way to the surface, I blink until my vision is cleared. Upon breaching, I'm forced to dive back under because of the burst of fire coming straight toward me. Blinking the pain from my eyes, a dark cave opening promises a safer break.

Coming up for air, I cough, gasping till my lungs are filled again. Quickly, I pull myself onto the cave floor, lying behind a large boulder. Not sure what the fuck that was, but I'm not dying today. The ground tremors. I grip my bow, knocking an arrow with shivering hands before quieting my breathing. Slowly sitting up, crouching behind the rock, peaking at the beast. A large, thick body covered in white scales, with blackened horns trickling along its spine. Its sinful red eyes and narrow mouth show off a row of sharp fangs opening to tease me.

"Come out, come out wherever you are." His tone is deep and coated with humor. I watch his eyes narrow into slights, reminding me of all the predators I've encountered on my hunts. It's a natural instinct once they find their prey. Not today, dragon. Today, I'm the predator, and you're my dinner. And what a feast I'll have. Knocking my arrow, I aim directly for its heart, unaware of the true anatomy of a creature that is supposed to be extinct. I'm guessing his heart is in the same place as any other animal. I read my release but stopped at the sound of another voice.

"Xiong, what are you doing in here?" Another dragon has entered the cave, paralyzing me with fear.

"Verglas, my dear sister, you are back." I blink a few times, watching the siblings interact with one another. The female, with a body covered in blue scales and brown horns, glares at her brother.

"And at a suitable time, I see."

"What? I was just trying to get you some dinner." He visibly shrugs at her, but her resolve doesn't falter.

"You may come out, my dear. No harm will come to you, I promise." Her eyes dart over to me.

She's talking to me. What the fuck is going on?

Hesitantly, I come out of my hiding place, knowing there is no other way out of here than to swim out. My arrow is knocked, aiming between the two of them. I tried to figure out which one would go down harder and decided on the white one, who I believe she called Xiong.

"The weapon isn't necessary." the female insists.

Not buying what you're selling.

"He tried to burn me up." I look between them. Xiong appears annoyed with him, picking at his teeth with a long claw. "You're not real. This is just an illusion due to frost illness or something."

Xiong growls. Verglas shifts into what I assume to be a passive stance. Lowering her entire body to the floor, trying to make herself seem smaller.

"We are very real, and neither I nor my brother will harm you." Her persistence, combined with my fatigue, has me slowly lowering my weapon.

"I am Princess Kaleigh, daughter of King Philip and Queen Anilla." Verglas respectfully bowed and gestured to her brother to do the same. Reluctantly, he submits.

"Xiong, don't just stand there. Make a fire so her highness can warm up." Verglas commands.

"Thank you." I watch in amazement as blue flames ignite the place, warming it and slowly melting the chill in my bones. Once I'm settled in a spot far enough away from them but not too far from the fire's warmth, the blue dragon walks over to a darkened part of the cave and settles in. I look over at her, trying not to stare. Xiong makes himself comfortable between the exit of the cave and the pool of water.

This is a new one. I wonder what the scholars will write. I wasn't only nearly eaten by dragons, but I was a prisoner of them. Do dragons usually toy with their food?

"So, what is a young Princess doing alone wandering the woods?" Xiong's question snaps me back to the present.

I think about lying but decide what harm could come of the truth. "I was traveling towards Ice Village on a mission sent from the Great Kings in the sky." My answer is short and to the point. The two dragons exchange a daunting look. "What is it that frightens you so? What is this mission?" Verglas asked.

"Answering a question with a question doesn't help," I told her. When neither of them responds, I sigh. "I was sent a vision of a strange man walking through this forest. I feel as though they were sending me an omen."

"Was this man hurting someone?" Verglas asks.

"I did not see, but I had a second vision and nearly drowned in my bath." Xiong burst out in laughter. Verglas snarls at him to be quiet.

"Ignore my brother. He is not always this rude."

"I have a younger sister. She kind of has the same personality as him." I bit my tongue, wanting to slap myself for admitting something so personal to this stranger." I started this quest not so alone, but I separated from my sister and our squire a few days ago."

"I can sympathize with the longing to be with my family. I am inclined to help if I can. Describe your visions. Perhaps I can help better ease your suspicions," she suggested.

"What is that going to do? Do you possess the knowledge to interpret their meaning? I don't know much about your kind, just that you're not supposed to exist."

"Yet here we are," Xiong interjects.

"Dragons have been gifted with many abilities. I have lived for many decades." I guess some insight couldn't hurt.

"There is a place in the castle called The Willow Well Garden. I went there some days ago to think like I usually do, and when I touched the water, it showed a man." I leave out the part about the pennyroyal before continuing. "He was traveling here in this forest." I try to reach her thoughts by the stoic look on her face, but I fail to no avail. "The last vision I had, he spoke and gave me some riddle. Follow the path before you now. A friend will be there to show you how."

Glancing over at her brother, who was now snoring, she finally spoke.

"Do you know the history of your people?"

I shake my head sideways before saying, "I know little, but what I can remember is this. Many years ago, there was a great dispute between kings before the barrier. My great-grandfather and the opposing king, Arnold Kawthorne, were about the betrayal of the dragons. They were all sentenced to die because of this."

I watched in terror as her expressionless face narrowed, her nostrils flaring as smoke began to spew from them.

"Lies! We would do nothing so dishonorable!" Xiong interrupts.

"Calm your scales, brother. Her knowledge is what she is taught." Verglas's calm tone deceives the scowl on her face.

I jump into a defensive stance, preparing for an assault or counter argument. "Lies? My family would never kill without a just reason!" My voice croaked, my chest heaving in and out as something wet dripped on my cheeks. I look up but see no ice.

"There is no need to cry. You will be educated soon enough." I touch my cheeks, realizing the water is coming from my eyes.

What the hell is wrong with me?

"Settle down, warm up and listen. You're safe here. I'll give you my word." Verglas reaffirms once more. Something about her has me obeying. I settle back down next to the fire. Arms crossed, face wet, and heart hurt. Verglas lightens up the mood by revealing the true meaning of my visions. "Do you know about the gift of sight?"

I wipe my face on my sleeve, curious about what she is asking and remembering something from school. "I believe I have read something about this somewhere. Why do you ask?"

She forms what I can only describe as a smile on her snout. "You do not realize the power that has been granted to you."

"I do not understand?"

"It has been quite some time before anyone has

been granted this gift. It is a heavy burden," she states.

"Are you saying…You think I have this gift?"

"I do."There is no hesitation in her confirmation. No lie in the depths of her eyes. My stomach churns in fear.

Even with the rising anxiety, I manage to ask, "Do you know the meaning behind my visions?"

"I have some knowledge of what they may be predicting." Silence overtakes the cave as I wait for her to elaborate. "Two paths will present themselves to you. One is a path of unity and strength. The other is betrayal and destruction. Do not repeat the same mistakes as your Greatest Grandfather."

"What do you mean?"

"I have said enough on the matter. It is all up to you." I move to protest, unsatisfied by the answers given to me, but I'm interrupted by the movement of Xiong marching to where his sister lay. "Come here, girl." Xiong growls.

I make my way over towards them. Three large eggs sit perfectly on a bed of straw. Two matching their uncle in color. The third is a mixed color of purple and blue. "These eggs are the last of the Ice Dragons," Verglas whispers, nuzzling them.

"There yours?" I ask, fascinated by the sight of this unbelievable experience; it temporarily renders me speechless. Verglas's eyes gaze proudly upon her offspring.

"You may feel them, so you know they are real." I smiled at the sense of humor.

I step forward, cautious but curious; as I put my hand on the runt of the three, a small pulse greets me.

Embracing the blissful feel of the unknown, my

eyes close. The ground below me disappears, and the feel of hard violet scales saddle between my legs. A warm breeze within a blue sky and white clouds dance around us. A majestic beast acts as my steed. Soaring through the air, I am at peace.

"I have never experienced something so incredible in my life."

"What did you see?" their mother asked.

It was difficult for me to form the words, but when they did, it was as if I actually lived it. "I was soaring through the air on the back of a dragon. Nothing but the clear blue skies for miles. I'm not sure, but I had the feeling I knew it. Its purple scales were glistening in the rays of the High Sun. I thought I might be scared. I wasn't."

Xiong gives his sister a disapproving look, making me wonder if it was an omen, too. "What is wrong?"

"My daughter, Azula, has given you a vision. One day, you will understand your gift. You are young, for now; listen to my guidance. Unity and love over violence and betrayal. Heart over mind." I took her words to my soul, coming to terms with the truth in front of me.

Something is happening. Dragons are back, visions are being sent to me and now, I know I need to get back home.

After the meeting with the eggs, I sat down and ate the rabbit I was provided with. For the first time since yesterday, I felt safe enough to close my eyes.

Just as I was hoping, the man was there. "Who are you?"

"Soon you will see. Once we meet, you and I are-"

"How will I know?" I interjected, trying to stay in

control but the dream shifted. He faded away, and a circle of fire engulfed the surrounding area.

"Kaleigh!" Abby's voice cut through the fog.

"Abby? Abby, where are you?" I can hear her crying out for help. The flames are too high, coating the air with black smoke. A name came across my head, something I recognized. "Azula!" I yelled, seconds later, a burst of cool air doused the fire. Azula appeared before her, a fully grown dragon, more beautiful than the vision.

"I will always help you, Kaleigh."

"What happened? Where are we?"

"This is what will happen if you choose the wrong path."

Chapter Eight

Rowland

It has been a few hours since I left Verglas's cave, the surrounding forest did not seem to change its scenery throughout. Tall trees draping over each other, the translucent snow hugging the ground, and speckled green bushes every few feet. If I weren't knowledgeable about the direction of travel I needed to take, then I would get lost here.

On the path ahead, I stop momentarily when the smell of burning wood hits my nose. Looking at the sky, I spot white smoke coming from nearby.

It's none of my business. Keep moving.

"You need to sit down!" A woman's voice echoes.

"Ignore it," I tell myself.

"We need to find her," the male responds. Then a scream of pain coming from him has my feet moving towards them. The closer I move, the louder their voices get until I set my eyes on them. The female is small, younger than me by at least three years. She's hunched over the man, batting his hands away while mending a wound.

"Tristian, you need to eat. My sister will kill me if I let you die."

"No, we need to go back for her." The man has a pale face with red-cut cheeks and a bruised eye. His efforts to stop her are useless.

They don't see nor hear me, which indicates they have no survival awareness skills. I step forward, my damn moral telling me to help them, and a branch cracks. Announcing me to them and every animal within the vicinity.

The woman swirls, her long auburn braid swinging as she positions herself between me and the injured with her blade in hand. "Get Back!"

I raise my hands in a position of surrender before saying. "Easy, milady. I mean you no harm."

"Then you should turn your back and leave," she snaps.

A groan comes from behind her, but her position doesn't falter. She's brave, I'll give her that. But her stance tells me she's had zero battle training. A thought crosses my mind and I speak. "You guys need help?"

"No. You just be on your way," she barks. Her eyes are narrowed telling me she's serious. Her hands are shaky but she doesn't back away. "Unless you're a healer, we need nothing from you."

"I am no healer, but I have healing herbs that will help your friend." The young woman's eyes lit up with intrigue. Slightly turning her head, barely enough to monitor me, the young man gives her a nod of approval.

"Very well. Remember, my blade is sharp and eagerly awaiting its next victim." Reaching into my sack, I grab some red-speckled leaves and cloth bandages. Cautiously approaching them, I place the supplies on a log across from them before stepping away.

Blade in one hand, grabbing the herbs in the other, her eyes never drifting, she quickly applies them to the injured man.

Her eyes soften when they meet the man. "How are you feeling?"

"The pain is easing. Thank you, kind sir," he says to me, but his gaze never leaves hers.

This is awkward. "You are welcome. My name is Rowland."

"My name is Tristian, and this is–"

"Abby, just Abby," she interjects.

I take my position against a fallen tree, leaning backward to give them a safe distance. "So, what happened to you, Tristian?"

Abby sheaths her dagger, keeping her hand at the ready. "We were attacked," she answers shortly.

"By what? A beast?" Another polar bear might be nearby but I imagine the damage would be greater than a few scrapes and bruises.

Abby moves to the other side of Tristian while he answers me. "Have you ever heard of the Red Griffin Bandits?"

"I can honestly say I have not." Curious to know if it was the same men that attacked me before. Given the red bandana with the griffin emblem.

"A terrible group of five criminal brothers. Known for their murderous nature," Abby states.

Tristian continues to elaborate. "They each bear the mark of griffin and wear a red garment upon their heads." A tremor runs down my spine at the flash of a memory. Silence overtakes them, and an awkward feeling lingers in the air.

I need to get moving. Perhaps these people know how I can get to the king. Those herbs can work quickly. Perhaps another few moments and he'll be better, then my conscience will let me leave.

"Tristian,"—his eyes snap from Abby to me— "some time has passed. Let us see your wounds."

Sitting up with help from Abby, he answers. "I am feeling a lot better." The cringe in his face betrays his words. "I am slightly hungry now."

"Healing herbs work that swiftly?" Abby questions. The glint in her eyes goes dark for a moment. She's cautious of me. I don't blame her. It shows me how smart she is.

She reaches into her bag, and I remember her question. "They can have wounds like his. A deep gash or fatal one would take longer or not work at all." Abby shows Tristian the few berries and acorns she must have gathered prior to our meeting.

My stomach hurts from hunger. I don't ignore it even though it means I will need to share. By the looks of them, they will need someone like me to help get them out of this place. Reaching into my bag, I pull out some frosted bear meat.

"Where did you get this meat from?" Abby asks, her voice piqued in intrigue.

"I didn't steal it, if that's what you're asking," I quip. When she doesn't laugh, I smile. "Does it matter? Really, this meat will feed all of us. Tristan needs more than a handful of grub to get better."

"Thank you for your kindness, Rowland. I am sure I would be dead if it weren't for you." Tristian's eyes sear into Abby's, pleading her to accept. It's humorous the way these two interact. Nothing like I've ever encountered before.

"I would hope you would do the same for someone else in need. I will gather some wood for the fire. Then we can eat and you can rest." I push to my feet to begin gathering up some branches, stones, and cloth. After a few moments, I've got a good fire going and the leg begins cooking.

"How is it you know how to do such things?" she asks. Her scornful eyes only leave me to check on Tristian's wounds.

"My father taught me when I was a child." Not a lie. "If I were ever lost in the forest, he wanted me to know how to survive until I found my way home."

"We are not lost," she says defensively.

"I didn't suggest you were," I respond but in doing so, I've pissed her off. She stands before storming off into the opposite direction of the High Sun, her curses fading along with her.

"Don't mind her, Rowland. We have been put through hell these last couple of days." Turning the meat, each gust of smoke fills my mouth with water, and my stomach with increasing hunger.

"I can only imagine." I pause a moment to think about asking a daring question. Perhaps these two are locals. I don't know why they are out here but it doesn't appear to be due to a lovers tryst. Cautiously, I speak. "Do you know how to get to Orion Fortress?"

"Unfortunately, no. But we wouldn't head in that direction even if we did."

A hum vibrates in my throat. "Why not? Is that not where you come from?"

Suggesting that could've been a mistake if I knew it wasn't true. "It is. However, we are waiting for someone. We got separated from her the night of the attack."

"You expect this person to still be alive?"

"Of course. Kaleigh is highly resourceful. She is the reason we escaped."

How can one woman evade five men? I struggled with it myself. Kaleigh, did he just say her name? Could it be?

"Our food is just about done. I would like to hear more about this amazing woman. How did you two come to be out here, and for you to tell me how she saved all of you."

"Her skills are unmatched. She strategically came up with a plan for us to evade them, and then she sacrificed her escape for us. I mean, she didn't get captured but she led the men astray while Abby and I got away." Taking the roast off the fire, and placing it on top of a cold stone, a loud sizzling sound was created.

"That looks appetizing." Tristian groans.

Taking my blade from my boot, I slice it into three even portions. With every cut, the juices seep down onto the stone, and Tristian scrounges up some energy to limp over to me. Without exchanging words, the expression of joy and gratefulness shines on his face. Once we are settled, I take my first bite. Juice rolls down my mouth, coating my chin but I don't care because it's tangy and perfectly roasted. A hint of burnt skin completes it.

Throwing the bones into the fire, Tristian looks around. "I wonder where she went off to."

Gulping some water, I say, "I am sure she will be back shortly. If not, I will go look for her."

"Very well. Should we build a makeshift shelter while we have daylight?"

"It will take some strength. How are you

recovering?" I know the herbs work quickly, and him replenishing his food will help, but I'm weary about letting him help build something.

"I have a dull ache. Since eating, I feel I can do some work."

"I will stay and help. But tomorrow I must press onward." He nods at my statement and we quickly get to work.

Tristian found some lashings for fastening, while I found some logs. Working together, we built a temporary frame and used the bear skin blanket I made to cover it. It was big enough for two people to comfortably lie down in. While rehydrating, we admired our work.

Walking in from behind them, carrying some fish, Abby breaks the silence in the air with a snarky comment. "I can see someone is feeling better."

Turning around, Tristian blushed when he saw her smiling at him. "We figured building something to cover us from the falling snow would help us get some much-needed rest."

Walking up to Tristian, Abby drops her catch of the day and hugs him tightly. Tristan whispers something in her ear, causing her to blush.

They're going to fuck.

Might as well offer to take the first night shift to let them have at it.

Releasing her grip from Tristian, turns toward me before speaking. Her usual scowl turned into an appreciative nod. "I appreciate all that you have done for us. But you understand that we are going to look for my sister once Tristian is ready for travel."

"I intend on making my way out tomorrow," I told

her.

"We need to do a watch rotation. Tristian, you will not take a watch. You need your rest." She kisses his cheek, before taking leave to the outskirts of the camp. Tristian's face is blushed, and he turns to take his rest.

" I will take the first watch," I say before she gets too far. She stops to turn back toward us. "Really, you need to ensure Tristan is settled. I don't feel keen on sleeping next to a man. No offense." I shrug it off.

"Fine." She sighs. I wait until they are tucked into the shelter before taking off in the far distance. I want to leave, but these people still need me. I wonder about her sister. Tristan called her Kaleigh. Could it be the same woman from my dreams? Verglas will know.

A couple of hours pass. Just as fatigue tries to take me but the last time I traveled back toward the camp, the sound of Abby moaning had me turning back away.

"Verglas, I need your help." With a flap of her wings, she appeared only seconds after she was called. "It is an honor to see you, my friend."

"Something bothers you."

"I have an internal struggle. I need advice."

"I sense confusion."

"I have met some people that need my help. My heart tells me to stay, but my head tells me to press on."

"The best advice I can give is to think about those who have helped you when you needed it most." Walking up to her, and placing my hand on her snout, I feel her reassurance. "I know what I must do but one more thing." She nods encouragement. "The man mentioned the woman named Kaleigh. Could that be her?"

"Only time will tell. Kaleigh is a rare name but

don't jump to conclusions until you meet her."

"She's lost. I intend to help them find her."

****

With Verglas's last words, I approach the campsite, aware of Tristian sitting outside, running a twig end through the ashes of the fire. Abby will berate me in the morning.

He doesn't flinch or look my way as I close the distance between us. As to not frighten him, I clear my throat, causing him to halt in his actions and meet my gaze.

"You seem distracted. Is it your wound? Should be nearly healed by now." I sit across from him, tossing some fresh wounds and dried leaves to the middle of the stone of circles. Picking through the ground, I find two stones and knock them together. A spark soon lights the fire once more. Warmth and the smell of fresh smoke engulfed us before he answered me.

"Anything to report?" He dodges my question by asking his own.

"Quiet as a field mouse." A smirk forms on his face as he finds my metaphor to be humorous. A moment of silence, a fatigued feeling and an enormous yawn escapes me, telling me it is time to rest. I avoid pressing my interrogation further so as not to lose any trust I have gained. Instead, standing and stretching before announcing my departure. "I am going to go to bed. You got the watch?" With a nod of assurance from Tristian, I finally enter the tent and eye the empty spot next to Abby. Laying on one side, appearing fast asleep, Abbygale has her blade cuddled in close quarters. Not that there is much room within this makeshift hut.

I move to lie down, but a sharp tip is pressed into

the seam of my pants. A little too close to my cock for comfort. "Keep this thing in check and we won't have any issues," Abby states, a slight glint of humor flashing in her eyes. I hold my hands up in a motion of surrender and she draws back.

As I lay down, she stood, leaving without another word.

After settling in, my eyes are heavy with sleep, and soon, the dream world takes me.

In the distance, a blue aura circles around the woman in blue. Swiftly, approaching her, I reach out but my hand goes through her. As if she is a spirit. A smile forms on her face. She fades into darkness yet again, leaving me with unanswered questions.

The ache in my lower back has me rousing before the scent of cooked meat hits me. I blink away at the bright rays seeping through the slit at the entrance. Sitting up, I look over and notice the other spot has recently been slept in. The vision from last night plays on repeat—it's more confusing than the last. Shaking away the fatigue and stretching out the pain, I rise, hunch over as I move outside, spotting my new companions engaged in conversation, oblivious to my presence.

"Good morning." My salutation does nothing to break their spell. I clear my throat, loudly and that seems to snap them out of it.

"Oh, good morning, Rowland. Did you sleep well?" Tristian asks with a smile across his face. They seemed in better spirits than when I first arrived. A swell of pride forms in my chest, knowing I played a small part in their survival.

"Very well, thank you." A lie. My body hurts like I

haven't slept in a bed in over a week.

"I must be off. I need to check the traps." With a kiss planted on Tristian's cheek, Abbygale darts off into the woods.

"It appears she is trying to avoid me." Still in awe of receiving a gift from Abby, Tristian's face is a rose-red color.

Completely ignoring my observation.

"I am sorry. Did you ask me a question?" He rubs the spot where her lips pressed against his, looking over at me still in a dazed stupor.

"I was actually just saying how I would like to know more about you two. How did you end up in this situation in the first place?"

Tristian's expression fell from happiness to wariness. Trepidation for fear he may close himself off from me as Abbygale has, had me elaborating further. "I suppose if we are going to be spending the next couple of days together, it would be best to acclimate ourselves to one another."

"I suppose you are correct. Just if you are honest with me. Agreed?" Tristian extends his hand in a motion of mutual respect and agreement. I clap mine against him, agreeing to his terms. "We grew up in Orion Fortress and we were simply traveling to Ice Village before the attack."

Why would they be traveling to that godforsaken place? "Do you often visit the village?"

He shakes his hide sideways before speaking. "No, not really. This would be the first."

"What started this visit?" My question spewed out faster than I'd hoped but curiosity won out.

Tristian's eyes narrow before one brow raises and

he says, "Listen, man, you sure are asking a lot of questions. How about you answer some of mine?"

I should punch myself for putting my foot in my mouth trying to avoid having to break a vow of honesty. Depending on the manner of his questions, I may be able to get away with half-truths. "Very well. What would you like to know?".

"How did you end up lost in the forest?" His right hand moves to another twig and he begins to trace the dirt at his feet.

Easy enough. "I was journeying to Orion Fortress to visit someone." I was going to that exact place to see the king but he didn't ask me to specify.

"Did you grow up there?" His attention was glued to the forest floor as we continued our talk which made this easier because withholding the full truth is easier when I'm not looking at his face.

"I can honestly say I did not. Tristian, what is the relationship between you and Abbygale?" This question caught his attention as he stopped his crafting of what I can only assume is a bird to look at me.

"What do you mean?"

The fear in his eyes tells me I've toed some delicate line. Instincts have me wanting to back off but the more I know about these two, the closer I will be to getting the answer about her sister. Is this Kaleigh the one woman haunting my dreams? "She has an affection toward you and obviously you to her. Yet, you are not married. The way you speak to one another is in a formality that is not common amongst peasants."

"We have mutual respect for one another, that is all. Besides, what would a loner like you know about the proper mannerisms of peasants?" The fire in his eyes has me flinching slightly. "I mean no offense but you don't exactly have the same demeanor of a low-born. You come from a noble family or you worked for one. Your tongue is far too respectful and educated."

A moment of silence passes between us before I look away and Tristian decides to reroute this topic to a different one.

"My parents died when I was just three years old. The king and queen took me in since I was an orphan. They truly are good people." Then why refuse to aid my people?

"I grew up with Kaleigh and we have become the best of friends. When you meet her, I am sure you will become friends." He smiles as if reminiscing about his departed friend. A look of admiration glinting in his eyes.

"You mentioned the king and queen—how do you know the two sisters? Are they connected to the king and queen? Did they work at the palace too?" I'm treading on thin ice now. But the poke for information doesn't seem to bother him. Not like the one about his relationship with Abbygale.

"It's complicated. How about you? Are your parents still around?"

"Mother died during my birth. Father became distraught for a while and had some resentment toward me. Gregor, my older brother, stepped in to take care of me and our father until he passed almost ten years ago." Something we have in common. Both orphans, stuck in a forest, chasing after daft dreams and ideologies.

"What's wrong with you two?" Abbygale's voice snaps our attention back to her. Upon her back was a medium-sized rabbit. It will make an excellent meal for the three of us. Loverboy stands almost immediately to embrace her but it becomes awkward when she slings the dead creature into his open arms.

"I see you have brought lunch and dinner. Let me take that from you." Tristian covers up his hurt by accepting it but when he takes another step, he stumbles over a low-hanging branch. I catch him by the belt just before his face is licked by the flames.

Once he is upright again, his face is flushed with embarrassment. The rabbit drops to the floor and Tristian takes off into the forest, leaving a confused Abbygale with her mouth hanging agape. "What just happened?"

I scoff. Shaking my head side to side before picking up the rabbit and carrying it to the skinning rock, which is just a large boulder.

"If you have something to say, then just say it." She places her hands on her hips.

"It's not my place," I mumble but that doesn't seem to get across to her because she closes the distance.

"What isn't?" Ignoring her, I unsheathe my knife and begin working on our meal. Her tiny hand darts out, gripping my wrist hard enough to catch my attention. "Tell me."

I meet her gaze, letting out a huff of breath. "The man has feelings for you and he just embarrassed himself in front of you. From what I have seen and heard since meeting the two of you, I'd say the feelings are mutual. Although, maybe he doesn't think so."

Jerking my hand away, I begin working once more. Need to preserve the coat as much as possible because it can be used for other things.

I don't see her fist coming but I feel it as soon as it cracks across my jaw, knocking my head sideways. The metallic taste of blood develops in my mouth. I spit my bloody saliva to the floor and turn back toward her. "You don't want to fight me, little girl."

"Oh, I think I do." Another punch only this time I catch her wrist, then her other one, spinning her around until her back is to me. "Let go of me."

"This is your only warning. Back off," I growl in her ear. She stops struggling and nods. I let her go and turn away from her.

"Where are you going?" she yells after me.

"Fuck off," I snarl back.

That stupid little girl. I could have killed her. I should. You fool, if you kill her, your people are surely doomed. Making it to the clearing was my new focal point. Speaking with someone sensible will help."Come here, dragon! We must discuss this at once." I don't like the sound of my own voice. Demanding a creature of majestic beauty and honor. But something must be done. I need something to give me hope that this is still the right path for my people.

"What happened!?" Her concerned voice flows through my head but my mind-eye doesn't see her.

"Where are you, beast!?"

"Calm your anger, Rowland. It is not wise to address me in such a disrespectful manner." My heart beat fast, face hot with rage, cheek still stinging from the hit, I calmed down enough to answer her.

"My anger is not directed toward you. That little girl hit me for no reason."

"Who do you speak of?" Her voice is calming. Like a mother to her child.

"Where are you? I hear you, but do not see."

"We are subconsciously connected. We communicate through our thoughts." I feel the rapid breathing in my chest begin slowing; I take my seat on a fallen tree.

"Verglas, forgive my brash anger. That is my brother, not me."

"You two are alike in many ways, Rowland. The anger burning in you is rooted in the same way as that of Gregor. Nonetheless, you are forgiven. Tell me about this girl."

"She is one of the two I am helping."

"She assaulted you. And you did not provoke it?" Her tone sounds like she is suggesting I did something.

"I may have said something offensive without realizing it. Another likeness I share with my older sibling," I say, throwing my hands up in defeat.

Her voice hums in my ears as though whispering in them. "You must make amends. It is the wise thing to do."

"Verglas, she is not the one from my dream. But there is a familial connection between the two. Could there be a connection?" She doesn't answer right away and it has me wanting to confirm everything. To reach into the dragon's brain and pull out all the answers to every question I've ever declared.

"The presence of the one you seek will overtake you.If this woman does not, then she is not the one."

"What does that mean? It sounds a bit cryptic. Don't these things just say what they mean without all the hidden riddles?" Her laughter bubbles forth, infectious, and I can't help but smile.

"A magic such as this is a powerful force that binds

two together. One man and one woman every few centuries will be given this gift when needed the most."

"I still do not understand what you mean."

"Once you are with her, you will."

Chapter Nine

Kaleigh

It was only a dream.

Cupping some water from the pool, I wash the sweat from my eyes. I stand and take a look around, seeing that it's just me and the nest of eggs. I placed my hand on Azuala's, smiling at the faint heartbeat radiating from her through my palm. "I will see you soon."

After my brief farewell, I pick up my weapon and exit the cave.

The outside light irritates my eyes as they adjust. I didn't notice either adult dragons perched above me until I heard Verglas's voice.

"Leaving so soon, are we?" Meeting her eyes, I watch as she tears into her breakfast, something I'm grateful not to be considered.

"I must be on my way. I need to find my sister."

"Xiong will escort you part of the way. And remember, princess, there are two paths for you to follow. Ensure you choose the one your instincts are guiding you down."

I nodded my understanding before looking past her to where the white dragon was sitting impatiently in the trees.

"Let us make way, girl," Xiong snaps. With one

last glance, I try to memorize this moment one last time, unsure of when I will see her again. Dragons were extinct as far as I knew, but now that I know they aren't, it's difficult to imagine not staying with them.

As we walked, the stillness of the air was only broken by the crunch of our steps on the ground. The snow isn't adequate for a covert mission. This silence is becoming too awkward and I know he doesn't like me very much, but the need to fill the little space between us is nagging at me.

"So, how far will you escort me?" His large left eye rolls. Something about humans really bugs this big guy. I want to know more, to break through the shell he clearly has around him but I know it would be useless. Xiong is the opposite of his sister. Cold, stoic, and frightening.

"Until my dragon eyes see the smoke," he grumbled.

"What smoke?" I squint my eyes to somehow zoom in further ahead of us.

"That smoke." Raising my hand to shield the sun's rays, it takes a few seconds, but then I see it. A small white cloud steaming from the ground between large trees.

"We will meet again, princess." Xiong takes his leave without giving me time to respond. His large figure was quickly hidden from the snow.

Following the path ahead, a familiar aroma of burning fire fills my nostrils. A smile morphs on my face as small flutters of excitement dance inside my stomach. I take off. Sprinting hard and as fast as I could just to be with her again. To know she is alive and unharmed. I'm so focused on that swirl of smoke, that I don't see him until I'm rolling on the ground, snow covering my hair. I jump to my feet, quickly drawing back an arrow and aiming at the masked figure. In my line of sight, I focused on a tall, dark-skinned man with brown eyes, wielding a steel blade.

"A sword and an arrow are not an even match. Perhaps a test of brute strength will determine the victor." His voice was unfamiliar and difficult to detect. He wears a cloth across his face, revealing only his eyes. Slowly and in synch, we lowered our weapons, placing them on the ground. If it's hand-to-hand combat he wants, then so be it. I've bested men larger than him because my uncle never let me think size mattered when it came to a fight.

As soon as our weapons hit the forest floor, we engage. With every punch and kick, I blocked and parried. The physical blows were full force. Hard and fast. His strength was more than I've ever felt. Blood dripped from my nose and mixed with my spit. Now standing face to face, his breath was coming as fast as mine. The smell of charred meat bellows out with his deepened breaths.

He was standing too close and I had one split second to take advantage of the small reprieve we gave one another. Kicking forward, I aimed to bring him down the one sure way any man would fall to their knees but instantly regret it. Searing pain and the cracking of bone followed as I doubled over, screaming, tears rolling down my face. I crawl away. Feeling pathetic but if I could just get to my bow. I reached out, my fingers just shy of the grip when a crack resounds in my head.

I couldn't move. My body was numb and I knew

this would be the end. The world was spinning, the sides of my vision closing in until darkness completely consumed me.

Warmth spreads through my body.

Is this what death feels like?

Something was off about this. I wasn't cold anymore, I smelled cooked meat, pine, and fresh snowfall. I attempted to open my eyes. The darkness was fading into a blurred vision of color. And then I saw her.

"Abby?" I croaked.

"Hello, sister." Abby smiles at me while pressing a warm cloth to my head.

"Is it really you?" She nods before leaning down to embrace me in the tightest hug I've ever been given.

"How did you find me? I mean, I was supposed to be the one to find and rescue you."

Abby chuckled, letting me go before placing the cloth down on the ground.

"You weren't too far from camp when you found our border. I heard a bunch of noise nearby. It sounded like fighting, so I came to help." Involuntarily, my hand goes straight to a bump on my head.

"Did you see who it was? Was it one of the bandits?"

"No, it was actually a friend. Well, he is more like Tristian's friend." She sighed. Fiddling with the hem of her shirt. What is she so nervous about?

"Who? If he is so friendly, why did he try to kill me?" I asked, trying to sit up. Abby helped me, holding onto me until my dizzy spell was subdued.

"Rowland didn't know who you were. And as you and I both know, it's difficult to know if the people in these woods are friendly. He's been ambushed before too," she explained.

I gripped her hand, trying to get control of my frustration for losing a fight and putting my sister in danger. If he wasn't a friend of theirs, he could've easily killed me and then them. I let out an exhale before asking, "Where is he? Is he here? Wait, who is Rowland?"

"He saved Tristian's life a couple of days ago. If it weren't for him, we would both be dead." She let out a heavy sigh, and for the first time, I noticed just how grown up she had become. Surviving on her own without me to guide her, and protect her, it's new and I know she had Tristian but...

"I see, and have you and this Rowland become close?" Was that admiration or appreciation I sensed coming from her? Something about the way she spoke about this stranger has me on edge. If she's fallen for him, then I'm more than ready to meet him.

A smirk formed before I saw pink rising on her cheeks. "No, he isn't the man for me."

"Well, let me go meet this Rowland. And where is Tristian?"

"I didn't want you to feel overwhelmed, so I made them wait outside. Plus, this shelter was only meant for two." Abby helped me to my feet. My head was pounding at first, and with every step, my right foot shot a sharp pain up my leg; but I was still eager to see Tristian again.

"You sprained your foot in the fight. Maybe I should just let Tristian come to you," Abby suggested, taking on nearly all my body weight.

"It's fine. I need to walk. It will help me feel better.

Besides, a sprain can get better in a few days. I promise to stay off it. Now, let me get some fresh air. This tent is suffocating." She laughed and it made me happy hearing that sound again.

"Kaleigh!" Tristian's face lit up as soon as he laid eyes on me. We embraced each other like old friends. He was thinner than the last time I saw him three days ago. He knows how to hunt, but I imagine out here, the food is scarce.

"I'm so sorry, Tristian." I wanted him to know how bad I felt about what happened to him. For leaving them to fend for themselves even if my intentions were good.

"What is there to be sorry about? I am alive."

"I shouldn't have let you come, neither of you," I said, looking between my best friend and sister.

"We've made out okay," Abby chimed in. I looked passed Tristian and finally saw the man who bested me. Limping toward him, Abby quickly put my arm around her shoulder to bear my weight again.

"Maybe you should question someone first before attacking them," I snapped. Keeping my cool with him wasn't going to go well. Who in their right mind just attacks someone without being provoked?

"Apologies, but the last time I let a man talk and not fight, I was nearly killed," Rowland explained but I didn't care. He kept his eyes off me. What kind of coward doesn't look someone in the eyes when talking to them? This wasn't going to go well. If he hadn't saved the two people I loved most in the world, I might have stuck an arrow in his eye.

"Look me in the face when I am talking to you," I chided.

"I need to go get more firewood." He cleared his throat, turned on his heels, and walked away. What a cowardly act.

"I will join you." I stumbled to the ground instantly. The pain in my foot was too much to endure. Abby and Tristian picked me up and brushed the snow from my clothes.

"I'm fine. I just need a little rest and I will be back on my feet in no time." Placing one arm across the back of Tristian and then Abby, I watched the stranger disappear in the distance.

Back in the tent with Abby helping me lie down again, we were silent as Abby unwrapped the bandage around my foot. My ankle was swollen and bruised. With the pressure released, I could feel the pulsating, and it made me bellow in pain.

Reacting quickly, Abby morphed a ball of snow in her hands and pressed it to my ankle until the pain began to ease.

Walking around a familiar place, I see the Willow Well Garden again. The flowers are in bloom and I notice someone sitting by the well.

"Mother?" I ran to her but when I reached out to embrace her, she vanished. The Willow Well was damaged, and the garden was gone. A new shadow appeared in front of me. "Who's there? What have you done with my mother?"

"Princess Kaleigh Orion, it's time to accept your destiny."

"How do you know my name? Who are you?"

Darkened green eyes appeared high above the shadow.

"Accept him, or this will be your fate."

I jerked awake, the pain in my head intensifying with the motion. There is a waterskin next to me. I lift it and swallow a large amount. The smell of cooked rabbit wafts into the tent and my stomach growls in response. I look around and notice a small plate with cooked meat sitting on top of it. With a small bite of breakfast and a gulp of water, I already begin to feel better. I look up from my food as my sister walks inside.

"Hey, sis, how are you feeling?" she asks as she touches her palm to my head. She's checking for any sign of a fever. Something we've seen the healers at home do many times before.

"I'm feeling a lot better now. I need to speak to him."

"To whom? Tristian?"

I shook my head sideways before answering. "No, Rowland."

"Sis, what's this about? I promise you can trust him."

I shrugged, unsure if I should tell her what I was suspecting. An accusation as big as that needs evidence and confirmation before I say anything. If Rowland is who I think he is, then Tristian's new friend might not be so trustworthy. "I need to speak to him about what happened."

"Once he gets back from his night patrol, I will send him in here. Promise me you won't kill him."

"I give you my word, sister's honor."

Chapter Ten

Rowland

"My sister requests your presence in the shelter." That's the greeting I get from Abby. It's better than the usual brush-off or scowl she's been giving me. I expected more hatred from her because of what I did to her sister. Perhaps I was wrong, she wasn't reasonable. Not that my haste actions are excusable. "Should I be worried?" I asked, stopping just before the diminishing pile of wood.

"Don't try to kill her, and you should be fine," she replied before turning her attention back to Tristian. Does her sister know about them? That's none of my business.

"Right." I set down the firewood and walked toward the entrance of the shelter. I let out a nervous exhale before entering.

"You asked to see me?" She appeared started because she immediately stood, knocked her head against the hanging branch the tent was draped over, and nearly fell over. I caught her, just before she face-planted. My hands were on her hips, hers gripping my biceps—we were frozen in that moment. Her eyes connected with mine.

She broke the little trance and said, "Yes, thank you. I wanted to apologize for the part I played in our fight."

"You were just defending yourself; I should be the one to apologize for acting first without thinking." I helped her to sit back down, cautious of her ankle. We were both silent for a few heartbeats. Both of us were unsure what the other wanted to say. She's very beautiful and matches the woman from my dreams perfectly. If I make the wrong assumption about her, then I might not make it out of this alive.

"Rowland, I just wanted to thank you for what you've done for my sister and Tristian."

"I believe they would do the same for me." She nodded in agreement before continuing to speak.

"This may sound kind of strange, but I need to ask you something." She appeared nervous, fiddling with the ends of her long brunette braid. Her eyes were wide, bright, and mesmerizing. Even with the few cuts and small bruises from our fight. I could see the beautiful woman underneath it all.

I answered her before my staring became too noticeable. "Interesting way to start. But I may have an answer."

"Have you ever heard of the gift of sight?" Why would she ask me that? Unless she has it too and I'm correct in who I believe she is.

"I have. Why do you ask?" I needed to know if she was getting the same visions as me. Did she know what it all meant? And if she could tell me what we're supposed to do in order to save this world.

"Hypothetically, if you knew someone with this gift and they told you they have had visions of you, how would you react?"

"Hypothetically speaking, of course. I would

simply ask what that person meant."

"Okay, again, this is all theoretical. If this person had dreams of meeting you and you told them little riddles and said we were each other's destiny, would that help?" It is most definitely her.

"I would say, I have had similar dreams about you too." She looked away from me, down at her hands, then back to my eyes.

"Are you saying hypothetically or realistically?" I watched her swallow.

My answer would confirm her suspicions of me just as her questions did for me. "Kaleigh, I have had visions of you these past nights and I believe, well, I think you are trying to say that you have too. That somehow we are connected with this gift."

"Verglas was right," Kaleigh mumbled under her breath.

"You have met the great Ice Dragon?" I asked, just to be sure I heard her correctly.

"Yes, and her ill-mannered brother, Xiong."

"He wasn't there when I was. What do we do?" I asked.

She pondered my question, most likely trying to come up with the correct one just like I was. I had a feeling we were both new to this and didn't know exactly what the right thing to do or say was. "I think we should be honest with each other. For some reason, we met. I saw you walking through this forest, so that is why I came to find you, but you say you saw me. How did you see me exactly? Where are you from?" If I told her I was from the kingdom of her sworn enemy, how would she react? Was she a loyal citizen of Orion? To the royal family? Verglas's voice rang in my head.

Honesty is the best way to approach this. Whatever happens, is meant to be.

"I was in the Obelisk Library back in my castle when I went through a hidden door that led me here. I ended up in–"

"Wait, we don't have an Obelisk Library in Orion Fortress. Who are you? Really? And what do you mean by my castle? There are none on this side of the barrier." What did I just walk into? No time to retract now that she heard it.

"I am Lord Rowland of Zoldir." The response from her was unexpected, to say the least.

With a widening smile across her face, she says, "I knew it. Your mannerisms and appearance are far too high class for a peasant. Why have you come here?"

"I am on a mission to seek an audience with the king. That's what my original purpose was. Until I learned about this gift and met a dragon."

"What mission?" she inquired.

"My brother, King Gregor, informed me that our life source, this magic, is fading. If we don't restore it, our world will cease to exist."

"How is my father, I mean the king, supposed to help?"

"You said, Father. That means, can you help me? You're the princess, are you not? You could convince him to see me. To hear me out rather than sending a hawk to refuse to come to our aid once more."

"I am. Why would my father refuse to help you? I don't understand." Her brows furrowed as she tried to figure out what was going on. Was she not involved with her court's business?

"Rowland, tell me how long your brother has been

asking for aid?"

"He told me he has sent five messenger hawks within the last couple of months." In response to that, she wobbles to her feet, I reach for her but she brushes me, limping toward the exit. I follow her and tell her the last of it. A warning. "One more thing. My brother plans to invade if he doesn't receive an answer soon."

Chapter Eleven

Kaleigh

I marched out of the tent, seething at his confession. He's from Zoldir. The territory is known for its ruthless nature. I should've known from that first vision that he was the enemy.

My fists are curled at my sides and I have to warn them. As soon as I see them, hand in hand, their noses touching, it only fuels my fire. They don't notice me at first but Abby takes two glances in my direction before separating herself from Tristian.

"Kaleigh, what's wrong?" She thinks I'm mad about her and Tristian. That can be addressed later.

"Remember the visions I told you about?"

"Yes, that is why we are out here," she responds. I look between her and Tristian before I hear Him.

"It's you?" Abby questioned. Putting two and two together.

"Yes," I hear him say.

"So, are we just going to stand here just staring at each other all day?" Tristian asks.

"We need to get back now," I command. Not wanting any of them to protest. I begin gathering up things, ignoring the pain in my foot as I go.

"We can wait another day. What's the rush? You still need time to heal," Abby said, reaching for me.

"It doesn't matter if we don't have a home to return to."

Abby looks toward Rowland. "What does she mean? What did you say to her?" When he doesn't answer her right away, I whirl around to face him.

"Tell them. Tell them what you told me. How you are the Lord of our sworn enemy. How your brother plans to invade us? Answer her, Lord Rowland!" I didn't realize I began crying until I felt the sting of coldness on my cheeks. I was hopeful after what Verglas told me. He was supposed to help me reunite the realm, not destroy it.

"Kaleigh, please calm down. I will stop the invasion. I just need to get a message to my brother," Rowland pleads but I ignore him.

"It may already be too late. I didn't trust you and now I never will. You lied to my sister, to Tristian about why you were here. If you'd just been honest…"

"If I would've been honest? You mean three days ago when I met them. Just tell them I'm from the other side not knowing who they were. What would they have done to me?" His reasoning sounds logical but I'm too angry to care. "Besides, there's no way Gregor figured out a way through the barrier."

"You did. What if he sends his armies the same way you did?" I narrowed my eyes on him.

"Kaleigh, what do you know? Have you seen something?" Abby asked. I hated hearing the fear in her voice. Ripping her moment of happiness away with unmasking this man's deceit.

"My latest visions have been anything but pleasant. Our mother…" I pause, trying to hold back tears. While calming my shuddering breaths.

"She's there one minute and gone the next. Then a beast with glowing green eyes appears. The Willow Well garden is destroyed. All I see is fire and death. And him."

"Kaleigh, I don't wish for war amongst our people. Tell me how to get to a village so I can send a messenger hawk to him." His eyes are pleading, but I can't trust that he won't send the wrong message. Tell his brother how he came to be here. Aiding in the death of my people.

"We need to get moving if we are to stop this war," I tell them and continue to pack in silence. The others got the hint that I was done with arguing and followed my lead.

I finally found him, and he's my enemy. If there is no war, there is still a chance of saving Orion. Even if it means killing him to do so.

Once they were packed and ready to move, Tristian handed me a makeshift crutch, made out of some branches, to help me keep the weight off my foot. It isn't ideal if we are attacked again. But I trust Tristian to protect my sister and I can handle whatever comes my way.

Tristian and Abby were at the front of the group, conversing with one another, hand in hand. I'm not too sure how I feel about them coming together. I'd want to hear more about it when all this war talk calms down. But I can be happy for them both. Tristian and I would've never worked anyway. He wanted more than a hookup and I was never ready, still not ready, for a bigger commitment.

After an hour of traveling, I needed to stop and rest for a few minutes. The crutch helped, but my arms grew tired, and the tree branch was rubbing my armpit raw. Rowland approached me.

"Kaleigh, I'm sorry about all this. You wouldn't be here if it weren't for me."

"That is the most honest thing you've said," I snapped. I've never been this cruel to another person before.

He sighed. "What's going to happen when we meet with the king?"

I couldn't look at him without wanting to throw a punch but I did in order to let him know just how seriously in trouble he was. This man's fate rested in my hands. Whatever I did say to Father upon our arrival home, would either be Rowland's death or retribution. "I don't know. I suppose it depends on what the conditions are like back home. And what I intend to tell him."

"And what is that I might ask?" I lean up against a tree, eyeing him from head to foot, then back again until meeting his eyes. They are a shade darker than in my dreams. He's much more than I expected. Physically handsome, strong, and highly skilled in battle. Mother would deem him the perfect candidate for my husband. I, on the other hand, wish to know a man before I marry him. You can't marry a man you just met.

"I don't know. You will either be deemed a hero or a prisoner." Something flashes in the light behind him. Quickly reaching for my bow, I draw back on the arrow and aim directly past him. Rowland holds up his hands in confusion but realization hits him as soon as the tip of the blade presses into his trachea.

"You killed my brothers. Now I'm going to kill

your man." It was one of the surviving Red Griffin Bandits.

"I had no choice; they were going to kill my sister and friend. Plus, I saw you finish your–"

"Liar!" he yelled, tightening his grip on Rowland.

"Easy, your quarrel is with me, not him," I need him alive.

"No, he tried to slice my legs off in our brief fight, didn't you?" Rowland grimaced at the hot moist breath upon his ear. I needed to find where Abby and Tristian ran off to, remembering he had a twin with him the last time I saw him.

"Where is your twin? Is he too afraid to come out and fight?" I asked.

"Shut up! Because of you, he died. I have been tracking you ever since." The bandit snarled.

"I don't understand. I brought no harm to him." Keeping him distracted with conversation would give Rowland the advantage needed to overpower him. With his continuous inebriated rambling, I watched as Rowland noticed the slight loosen in grip and elbowed the bandit in the face. He fell to the ground, unconscious, blood forming on the cut on his lip. I grabbed Rowland's blade and prepared to stab the unconscious man in the chest.

"Stop!" Rowland said as he grabbed my hand.

"He has tried to kill us twice now."

"Don't you see? He already suffers from the loss of his family. Killing him will only relieve him of his pain." At that moment, I saw a new side to him. Merciful Rowland wants to save a man who would kill us rather than give him the death he rightfully deserves. Looking into his gentle brown eyes, the dip in my stomach catches me off-guard. A crunching sound mixed with giggling from Abby interrupts and breaks through our momentary bubble.

"Where have you two been?" Rowland asks, releasing his grip on me.

"Just looking around." Abby and Tristian's hair was a mess with leaves mixed in. Yeah, right.

"Who's that?" Abby asked as her cheerful expression faded.

"It's the last bandit we will have to deal with. Get some rope, he's coming with us." I stated while sheathing Rowland's blade. Rowland searched the unconscious man, relieving all the weapons he had on him, which was only one blade before binding his wrists.

"Shall we wait until he awakens?" he asks.

"No, you will carry him." I waited for the protest, but none came as he picked up the bound prisoner.

"Father will be pleased to know we have single-handedly stopped the Red Griffin Bandits. But I guess with an impending war, that will be the least of his worries."

Chapter Twelve

Rowland

With the passing of each hour, Tristian and I traded turns carrying the prisoner. Still unconscious, the only noise comes from his snoring and talking in his sleep. A loud groan came from Tristian and he dropped the man.

"What happened?" Abby asked.

"He, he started peeing on me." A look of disgust came across all their faces as we saw a wet spot on Tristian's coat.

"What the hell? Where am I?" the bandit asked, confused and groggy.

"Oh good, now he can walk to the fortress," I exclaimed.

"You can't keep me tied up. Let me go!" He tried to scramble to his feet and escape.

"There isn't anywhere in the forest that you can run that I won't be able to find you. You're going to be punished for all of your crimes." Kaleigh's voice was cold and stern.

I watched as his eyes widened in fear at her threatening tone. "Please, I repent. Let me repent."

"That is between you and the Great Kings of the past," Kaleigh said as she hobbled away. I helped the man to his feet, advising him to stay quiet. Tristian was still complaining about the pee while Abby continued to laugh.

"Tristian, you have a choice dear, freeze or deal with the smell. Be warned, I will not be kissing you until you bathe." Abby laughed and caught up with her sister.

All was quiet as the time passed along. Thoughts about Verglas and Gregor keep my mind occupied. What should I expect when I see the king? As dawn approached, we made our way onto the familiar cobblestone road which brought us all a sigh of relief.

"Following this path will lead us straight into the marketplace. We will be home by dark." Kaleigh yelled from afar. Maybe I can find that portal once again, but that would raise suspicion. How can I stop a war if I'm not here to do it? It could be anywhere among the trees, and I don't want to risk getting lost again. The bandit was still submissive and quiet, which worried me.

Is he plotting something?

Approaching the border was unlike anything I'd ever seen before. A clear wall of falling snow connecting the sky to the ground was mesmerizing. With each person passing through, they vanished to the other side. Entering, I felt an indescribable sensation pass through me. Once on the other side, the temperature rose to a comfortable degree. We no longer needed the warm coats, we took them off.

The vacant market was quiet. There was a street lined with vendor carts and behind that, a row of wooden houses. A stoned bridge arched over a trench of water connected to the castle roads. All of us eagerly crossed over, being greeted at the steel gates. The guards escorted us down the corridors to the throne room.

"Take this prisoner to the dungeon," Kaleigh ordered one guard. Before the guard leaves, a loud opening of the throne room doors catches our attention. My heart skips a beat as I see who enters the hall. The king and queen rush to their daughters with welcoming hugs.

"Where have you three been? I had the royal guard searching for days," King Philip said.

"I know, Father. It's a long story." With all the warm welcomes, I waited for my introduction.

"I see you have brought some company?" Queen Anilla asked, looking at me and then the bandit.

"Father, this is the last surviving member of the Red Griffin Bandits. We have captured him for you."

"To the dungeon until sentencing tomorrow." King Philip ordered. As the guard was exiting, a crooked smile came across the prisoner's face and just as I was about to say something, Kaleigh grabbed me by the arm.

"Father, this is Rowland Kawthorne. Lord of Zoldir. He asks for an audience with you." She surprised me with her smile and introduction. I was expecting her to send me to the dungeon as well.

"Lord Rowland, I know why you've come. But how have you crossed the barrier?" Stumped by the kind nature of his majesty, I look to Kaleigh for moment to gage how I should react but then look back towards the king. "It is late, everyone rest, and we will continue this discussion in the morning."

****

Kaleigh

I toss and turn all night. I guess I have gotten used to sleeping in the forest. Throwing my robe on, I peek out my door down the halls to ensure they're vacant before sneaking my way to His door.

What am I doing? Okay, leave now before it's too late.

I turn on my heel to make my break toward the corridor but I wasn't fast enough. My shoulder is jerked backward and soon I find my back pressed to the other side of his door with the tip of a blade pressed to my chin.

"Oh, it's you," he whispers.

I look at him from head to toe, my eyes catching the ripped corded muscle of his body until landing on his waistline. Thankfully he's wearing pants. I can feel the heat in my cheeks. Unsure if it was caused by embarrassment or my growing attraction for this man.

"What are you doing here, princess?"

"Uh, want to lower the blade?" I asked.

"Sorry." He backed away, putting it back under his pillow. "Can't be too careful when your in your sworn enemy's home."

"Right." I rub the back of my neck, too afraid to move any further inside. I try to come up with an excuse but instead blurt out something ridiculous. "I think we should get to know one another better."

I could slap myself for suggesting it.

Rowland turns to me. His face light in the shadows of the White Sun. "I agree. But first, your family needs to send aid to mine."

"I can't control what my father does, Rowland."

I rub my arms, ice kissing my skin as gooseflesh rises. Why do I feel so nervous right now? He closes the final distance between us leaving only a foot of space. I can feel the heat radiating off his body and I want to wrap myself in it like a warm blanket.

"I think you underestimate just how much control you can have over a man, princess." Wasn't sure how to respond, so I moved closer, the fabric of my bodice slightly brushing against his bare chest. "What are you doing here?"

It came out in a whisper. His husky tone made my knees quake. Breath quickens and mouth dries. The palm of his hands land on the door behind me next to each ear and he leaned his head forward, our breaths mingled. Was he going to kiss me? Did I want that?

"Don't make me ask again, princess."

I swallowed. "I just want to make sure the message is sent to your brother in time. There's no need for innocent blood to be spilled."

He smirked. His eyes searching mine for the half-truth I just told him. "Are you staying?" I raised a brow. Confused. "The bed is big enough for us both but I fear what might happen if you join me tonight."

I narrowed my eyes this time, gripped the knob and turned, causing him to stumble forward but he caught himself on the door. A chuckle vibrates in his chest. I didn't give him the chance to speak again.

****

The next day I invited Rowland to train while my father was working on the parchments we'd be sending over. I decided to look at myself in the mirror. Double checking that my white tunic was tucked into my brown pants nicely and that my boots were strapped up to my knees. My hair didn't have any flyaways and I applied a little bit of cosmetics.

"Wow. You really like this guy, don't you?" I turned around, startled at my sister's words.

"How'd you sneak in here? I usually can hear you."

She uncrossed her arms and sat on my couch. "I know." She looked at me, searching for something. "You do seem a bit more flustered since he joined our little group."

I blushed. "Yeah. Well, what about you and Tristian?"

"What about us?" I was avoiding this conversation by going into another one that I really didn't want to talk about. She let out a heavy breath."Look, I know you two had history and I'm totally cool with it. I don't need or want your permission or blessing or whatever you have going on inside that head of yours. Don't worry about my relationship until you figure out yours."

Abbygale did have a point.

We decided it was best to leave and head to breakfast before going to train. Abby wanted to start learning how to properly kill someone and evade capture. The events over the past week made her realize just how important throwing a dagger is.

Chapter Thirteen

Rowland

"Well, Lord Rowland, I'll be sure to include that in the message to King Gregor. I wouldn't want to spill innocent blood either," King Philip said while taking my hand.

And Gregor thought I couldn't resolve this with my diplomatic strategies.

"What's going on?" I knew it was her before I locked eyes with her. Kaleigh showing up was completely unexpected. She was in that lilac nightgown that always showed up in my visions of her. Those did nothing to justify the real figure though. My cock stirred with the sight of her and I knew I was doomed from this point on.

"For you and him to be married, of course," the king answered.

She looked between the two of us. I didn't move at Abby's gasp. Would she reject me? Or the idea of being married to me?

"Fine."

I blinked. "What?" How did she agree so easily? We barely know each other.

I didn't take my eyes off her as she strode over to where the king and I had been sitting and took her place across from me at the table. The tops of her boots knocked into mine and she buttered her bread avoiding eye contact. I nudge her to catch her attention. I need to know how she truly feels about this arrangement.

"Well, this is awkward," Abbygale announced before stuffing eggs in her mouth.

"Father, I'd like to invite Rowland to train with me today," Kaleigh asked. Still avoiding me and looking at the king.

Philip swallowed down his wine before agreeing with her. "Yes, of course." The king pushed his chair back, wiped his mouth clean, and excited the room without another word.

There wasn't much else said between the three of us. Only the scraping of utensils and sipping of juice was heard. But my new fiancé didn't need words. The dark blue daggers in her eyes did the trick. She was pissed. Not sure if it was at me or the new arrangement she walked into.

****

After breakfast, they led me to the courtyard where the training gear was. At the center looked to be a marked sparring area. I went to grab a sword but she stopped me. "I think we should hand-to-hand."

"Because that went so well last time," I stated.

"My sister wasn't there to see my mistakes. She wants to learn and I intend to teach her. Are you afraid I'll win?" She challenged, smirking at me.

This should be fun. "Lead the way, princess."

Kaleigh wrapped her fists in white cloth before entering the arena. I followed suit knowing the purpose was for protection.

She got into a fighting stance, her eyes narrowed and focused. Different from our first unconventional meeting. I caught her off guard last time. This was a side of her I'd never seen but anxious to know more about.

"Don't go easy just because we know each other," she spat.

"Wouldn't dream of it, princess."

Her small figure moves with grace as she charges for me. I dodge her first punch but didn't expect her foot to catch my side so easily. I wince but grip her thigh in a vice. She spins out of it, kicking me in the gut, causing me to double over in pain. "Fuck."

"Get up, Rowland. I know you can fight better than this."

I meet her challenge by tackling her to the ground, the sound of her back hitting the pad sings in my ears. I have her wrists pinned with my hands and the weight of my body has her hips cemented in place. She bucks up causing her to rub against my cock. I leaned forward, teasing her with a nip at her ear, knowing that lighting my weight would give her the chance to roll us. Just as I predicted, I'm on my back now and she's in the position I desperately wanted to see.

What I didn't expect was the searing pain and taste of iron in my mouth from the punch she landed on my right cheek. Another one comes, but I catch her again. Then the other makes us roll once more.

"Give up, princess. I'm much stronger than you are. You'll never be able to overpow–"

"Are you sure about that?" The tip of an arrowhead gently touches my neck.

"That's cheating," I stated, amused.

"I call it winning. Now, are you going to treat me like a real opponent or am I going to have to explain to my father why we have to ship your lifeless body back instead of a parchment?"

I thought for a moment she was kidding, but she pressed the jagged edge into my skin, cutting me. That's when I knew she was serious. I released her and exited the courtyard. "Coward," Kaleigh shouted at my back.

****

Kaleigh

"Bastard can't even treat me with respect," I muttered watching him leave.

"Why'd you do that?" Abby asked.

"Do what?" I pretended not to know while unwrapping my wrist. I took the chance to grab Shadow Striker and practice aiming at the targets five-hundred yards away. The first one hit.

"He didn't deserve to be treated like an enemy."

Second one center. "He is one."

"Not anymore. You're to be married remember?"

The last one didn't hit. "Back off, Abby. I don't know why everyone is so trusting all of a sudden."

"He saved mine and Tristian's life. Or does that not matter to you?" I didn't answer her. Ignoring that fact. "What happened to you in those woods?"

I looked to her, finding her bright blues filled with concern. "Nothing."

Chapter Fourteen

Rowland

The next week was rough. Adjusting to life here while Gregor and Philip corresponded with one another. Only two hawks have been sent and none received. Not to mention Kaleigh was giving me the cold shoulder.

I was determined to change her attitude toward me. Tonight, the heir of Orion would become more than my enemy.

When everyone else headed to bed, I made my way outside her window. Picking up some small pieces of gravel, I began throwing them to make noise. It took a few tries before she was aiming her arrow at me.

"Rowland? What the hell are you doing down there?"

"Dear princess, please join me for a midnight stroll." In the pale White Sunlight, I swore I could see her eyes roll.

"Why should I?" Her snark was becoming one of the things I found most attractive about her.

"Because I'll let you win." I winked. Not knowing if she'd see it. She disappeared from my sight. I waited for a few heartbeats. Then a few more. Until I began to lose hope.

Then I heard her. "Catch."

I looked up at the last second. Her small body was

falling from the balcony. Without thinking, I reached out and caught her. But it was unexpected so we fell to the grass. Her laugh filled the serene air and I smiled back at her.

She gripped my hand to help me up before racing me to my horse. We saddled, her in front of me and I tucked her ass perfectly into my groin. I wrapped my arms around her waist while she took the lead.

We trotted along a small river, until going down a heavily used path that led into the Elkon Forest.

When we stopped, she got off and tied the horse to the base of a tree. Her back was to me and I hesitantly approached her, gripping her hips to spin her.

"Why?" she asked.

"Did I ask to marry you?" She nodded. "Because, princess, there's no one I'd rather spend the rest of my life with than you." I captured her lips, pulling flush against me. The moment was over before it began because she stepped away from me, holding her hand to her mouth.

"I'll marry you, Rowland. If it means peace between kingdoms but I'll be your wife in name only." I raised a brow in question. "That is the first and last time you lay your lips on me."

****

Kaleigh

Rowland avoided me, only speaking to me when necessary, for the next month. It was as I expected. I was too young to commit myself to him. Once this war is over, I'll be leaving. Exploring the western side of the realm. If it exists.

Tristian and Abby grew closer. Our parents didn't seem bothered that she was in a relationship with a servant. I guess by saving her life it earned their respect.

"What's wrong with you, darling," Mother asked me as I was sitting in my bachelorette room. It was where everything for my impending wedding was held. Today they were fitting my gown.

"Nothing."

"A princess should smile when choosing her wedding dress. It will be the best and most memorable day of your young adult life."

"I highly doubt that, Mother."

She gritted her teeth. "Why have you been so rude to him." What? "Don't look at me like that. Lord Rowland. He's been nothing but a gentleman since stepping into our castle."

"If you like him so much, why don't you marry him."

She looked to the sky for a moment as if to imagine it then shook her head. "That's ridiculous."

"Right."

"Your sister thinks you two need to be locked in the same room for three months to work through issues. And I'm starting to agree with her."

I snapped to her, brushing the seamstress's hands away from me and taking my leave. When I made it to my room, I couldn't help but run to the bathroom as bile was rising in my throat. Nothing came out.

"Bad fish?" a deep masculine voice asked.

I looked up at the steam-coated-looking glass and realized I wasn't in my room. I turned around and saw him. All of him.

His bronzed skin was littered with years of training, but when I saw the rest of him, my mouth watered. The droplets of water still coating him had my tongue dancing with the anticipation of what he tasted like.

"I'm sorry," I whispered, and he moved closer to me.

My eyes dropped but he caught my chin, forcing them back up to his. "You have nothing to apologize for."

I couldn't fight it anymore. I didn't want to.

My hands moved on their own accord. Gripping his biceps and moving up to his neck before I raised on the tips of my toes and pressed my lips to his. "I thought you said—"

"I lied." Our kiss deepened. Heat engulfed me. His hands gripped my ass lifting me to sit on the counter. I wrapped my legs around his waist, pulling him closer to me. Our tongues mingled and the rising lust for each other took over. His hands moved up until his fingers found me soaking.

I gripped his hard shaft, pumping him until I lined him up to my entrance.

"Are you sure?" he asked, breathlessly.

"Yes."

He kissed me before pushing in. I moaned and he muffled it with another soul-capturing kiss. My pussy clenched and stretched at the size of him. Tristian was small in comparison.

"Fuck, princess, you were made for me." I didn't respond because I felt the same way only not about sex. He moved in and out, slow at first, and then he picked up the pace. I dug my nails deep into his back, down to grip his tight ass. There were no more words. No more looks. Nothing but the sound of flesh against flesh.

Breathless kisses and racing heartbeats. I was close and I knew he was too.

Before he asked, I mumbled, "You need to pull out."

"Okay." He grunted. He picked up the pace, chasing my release and I clenched down, but he pulled out too quickly, spilling his seed all over my skirts. I didn't have time to protest as he placed his mouth against me. Sucking and licking. His fingers found my entrance, pumping them at a punishing pace as I rode his tongue until I felt my climax rise. My thighs closed around him, trapping him, not letting him breathe until I could move again.

When he got to his feet, our foreheads pressed together.

"You look ravishing," he said. "But isn't it bad luck to see you in that before we're married?"

"I don't believe in all of that."

He chuckled. "I think we should talk."

"Right. But I need to change."

"If I let you leave, promise me you'll come back to me." I searched for understanding but gave him a nod. He pulled me in to kiss me once more before letting me go.

I couldn't stop smiling the entire walk to my room. It was the right decision. Why did I wait so long? When I shut my door, I drew a quick bath and discarded the wedding dress into the dirty linens. I pulled on a dark blue gown and made my way back to his room. Only, I thought about talking to my sister about what happened.

When the door opened, it was her, only a sheet was pulled up to her neck and a smile was painted across her face. "Oh, I'm kind of bust, sis. Is it an

115

emergency?"

"No. Not at all." I wouldn't tell her until absolutely necessary. I wanted to keep what happened between me and Rowland. I'm still unsure that it actually happened.

I hesitated for a few heartbeats outside his door. Inhaling and exhaling, calming my nerves, I knocked. A loud crashing sound from inside the room prompted me to enter.

"Rowland?" The room is dark but one torch casts a small glow over him. Fear in his eyes is the first thing I see before noticing the black shadow covering his mouth.

"Run, princess, runaway!"As I call the guards, I run toward him, but he is swiftly taken out of the window and disappears into darkness.

"Princess, is everything okay?"

"No." I race to my parents' room, shaking them awake. They look at me with confused and sleep-deprived expressions. "Father, I am sorry to disturb you, but something grave has happened."

"Can it not wait till morning? Is it your sister?" he says, sitting up.

"The Lord is gone. He's been taken by something. Father, I saw a black shadow take him." The king jumps out of bed, throwing his robes on before following me to Rowland's room. We searched high and low with a few guards, looking for any kind of clue as to what kind of creature could take off with him.

"I've contacted the High Counsel. They've informed me the magic of this magnitude could only be conjured up by the darkest of creatures." Sir Palmer says. My uncle showed up just after Father and I made our way into the room. How could this happen? Were we followed? A thought crosses my mind. There was only one person who tracked us throughout that forest.

"Bring the prisoner here now!" I demanded, and after a few minutes, he appeared with the guards.

"My, my, look how pretty you look in your nightgown. Almost good enough to taste," he teased with his yellow teeth.

"What have you done with him?" I commanded.

"I'm sorry, you're going to have to be more specific?" In a flash, I pull a blade from the nearest guard and hold it to his throat."I will run you through right here, right now, if you don't tell me. What have you done with Lord Rowland?"

"It's too late. Where he is, you will never find him." A dark twisted look in his eyes tells me he isn't lying.

"Tell me or you will surely die!" Nonetheless, anyone is traceable. I can find him again, no matter where he is in this world.

"Toxic air bellows from the cracks in the ground but that isn't the worst part. It the Drakere you must worry about." I grab a fistful of his hair, making his neck taut as he looks at me and continues."If you attempt to go there, princess, even a skilled archer like you won't last an hour." His wicked laugh made my ears cringe.

"Why have you done this?"

"Don't you see? A war is brewing and soon justice will be served." He laughs.

"Tell me the name of this place. Now!"

"I will tell you. But you must take me with you."

"Out of the question!" Father intervenes, gesturing for a guard to subdue me. I step away, handing the blade over before the guard can touch me.

"Father, if we don't get Rowland to send a message to his brother, there will be a war." I watch as my father approached the bandit.

"Tell us where the Lord is, and I will offer you a deal on your sentencing."The bandit eyes the king, then me. "If she takes me with her, then I will tell you."

"Kaleigh will not be going on a mission as dangerous as this. But, I will allow you to go with my general to retrieve the young man." I went to protest but Mother pulled me to her, shaking her head to silence me.

We all waited on bated breath before he gave us the answer we were seeking. "He is where he is supposed to be. As you are where you're supposed to be." I leaned forward, wrapping my hand around his throat and digging my sharpened nails into his skin. Squeezing just enough to let him breathe and croak.

"Location," I demanded.

The bandit's eyes seemed to smile as he struggled to chuck while giving me the answer, "Hollow Realm."

Chapter Fifteen

Rowland

My head is pounding. What attacked me last night?
I pry my eyes open, and through blurred vision, I see a
spotted image of a beast standing before him. A gush of
freezing water flushes my eyes and face, making me
cough. My vision clears and I'm staring at a large man-
beast. I try to move to fight the creature, but quickly
realize my wrists and ankles are bound by iron chains
connected to a stone wall. I frantically search for her.
But revel in the joy of not seeing her here.

"Let me go. You have no right to keep me here."
The creature laughs in my face, spraying me with foul-
smelling spit, before placing a brown bag over my
head. I feel his rough hands grip my wrist before
releasing them from the iron chains, only to be replaced
with tight rope. The cloth draped over my head smelled
of rotten food. Through the thin linen, I get a small
glimpse of a vacant, narrow corridor that leads to a
spiraling staircase. Every ten steps, a molten candle
burns to light the way. A stabbing pain radiates through
my bare feet and increases when the exposed skin lands
on the hot stones.

"Pick the prisoner up and carry him from here." A
firm voice comes from the right side of us. The rough
hair of the beast's head scratches my exposed side,

reminding me of sandpaper, as I'm easily lifted and tossed over his broad shoulders. With each heavy step, my bound fingers nearly grip the edge of the bag. Stealthy, I slip the thin fabric through my index and middle finger and lift it slightly to glimpse my surroundings. A wooden bridge hangs delicately over a river of lava that gives off unbearably hot temperatures. Panic swells in my chest.

Once across the bridge, I'm forced to walk again. And I'm not sure if I prefer the hot stone or the furry beast. With one guard on either side of me, I turn my head to examine them the best I can through the screen in front of my eyes. I wager they are at least two heads taller than me. Although tempting, I don't believe I would stand a chance at making a break for it. We approach a vast arch on the side of a tall castle with five iron bars blocking our entry. With a blow of a horn, the gate is lifted, and we soon enter a barren courtyard. Down a desolate corridor are posted guards. Each is positioned in the tenth column, and I keep that in mind. This must be a prison with how particular this place is set up.

I stop when something sharp nicks my right heel. "Fuck!"

My shoulders are pushed forward."Keep moving."

We continued forward; I wince with each step, but I could see we were in a nicer room, and at the center front, there looked to be a throne. On either side of it, statues of dragons match Verglas in nearly every way. When the bag is removed, I sigh when a slightly cooler breeze kisses my skin. A door behind the throne opens, and a bald man dressed in robes comes in. He takes his place at the front and sits.

"Welcome, Rowland Kawthorne. I have been expecting you for quite some time." The man makes a gesture, and a servant brings him something to drink. "You are much smaller than I imagined."

"Well, you know what they say? Can't judge a man by his looks." I wait for a chuckle. Any sign that this man has a sense of humor. "Because if I were to make a statement based on your looks, I'd say you're one of the most idiotic men I've ever met. Taking the fiancé of a very powerful princess of a very powerful kingdom wasn't the smartest move."

He smiles this time.

"Release me at once! You have no right to keep me here. I have done no wrong against you!" I try to plead my case, but by the smile on his face, he appears to be unfazed. After wetting his lips, he walks toward me before digging sharpened nails into my jaw and lifting my head to meet his eyes.

"Oh, but I do, Rowland of Zoldir." His dark eyes dance with glee before I think about what I'm doing. My spit coats his face, and a searing pain across my cheek follows as the fist of one of the guards punishes me for my actions. "Hostility and disrespect are unnecessary."

"Why have you taken me prisoner? I have every right to know."

He releases his hold on me, turns away, and sits back down. "You are here because I want you here." A sinister smile of blackened teeth, clearly the result of practicing the dark arts, causes bile to rise in my throat and my stomach to churn. "You are here because of the treason you committed against me, your emperor."

"I have no emperor. Zoldir is ruled by my brother,

the king. Your accusations are false."

"I am your emperor!"His pale face is flushed with redness; clearly, this guy is easily offended. "I rule this world, and you committed treason when you saved the dragons," he states in a calmer tone.

"I've never saved a dragon in my entire life. There are none in Zoldir."

"Ah, but you weren't taken from your homeland, were you?" I averted my eyes slightly before meeting his challenging gaze once more. "I ordered every dragon to be killed, but you, or your foolish grandfather rather, rebelled and saved some."

"My great-grandfather was no fool. You have no right to punish me for the deeds of my ancestors."

"Seeing as he is already dead, you must take his place."

"You have no right to speak of things you do not know. You are delusional." If my hands weren't bound, I'd be curling my fist with my rising anger. The way my heart is thundering in my chest and blood is rushing through my ears, I am questioning my restraint. I've been mad at Gregor before but never felt like this.

"You don't know who I am, and I'll forgive you for your ignorance, seeing as your parents wouldn't have taught you about me. My name is Santana. I reign over Dalaria and all its followers. Lesson number one, little lord, blasphemy is not tolerated here. I am the emperor, and you will endure the punishment for treason. Once I am finished with you, I will march my armies into your precious Zoldir, kill your brother, and take over the land. And no one will stop me."

"You won't make it out alive." It was a bluff at best, but I'd never let my home fall so easily.

"Take him back to his cell." Santana walks back to his throne; as I'm being held away, I take the opportunity to get in the last words of this conversation.

"When I escape, and I assure you, I will. My sword will be the last thing you see before you die."

I'm rushed back to my cell and was given a pile of clothes to wear. The clothes are ragged with holes and stained with the blood of their previous owner. A pair of black boots have a repulsive smell coming from within. They smell of death, but I welcome them to cover my bare feet.

A small plate of food is pushed through a quant opening at the bottom of the prison door. A charred slab of bread accompanies a mound of yellow mush. The smell is off-putting, but I eat it to regain my strength. The mush is earthy and smells of sulfur, but it is not too bad mixed with the charred bread. A small cup of liquid water is quickly gulped down.

In my cramped four-by-four prison cell, the walls are bare, and consist of one door and a barred window, taunting me with its unreachable height. A small bed with no blankets is situated at the back. I sit upon it to assess my situation. What mess have we gotten ourselves into this time? Laying down, I let my eyes fall shut, and thoughts of *her* flood my mind.

Verglas appears before me, standing within her cave. Not the *her* I was hoping to see.

"Verglas, I need your help. I have been taken by a madman who is falsely accusing me of a crime I did not commit." Her empathetic eyes gaze upon me. "Speak to me. I need your help."

"My dear Rowland, you are in dangerous territory. Help will be on its way soon." Her image quickly fades as Kaleigh appears. She smiles, touches her hand to my cheek, and whispers in my ear, "I will find you." She's gone just as soon as she appeared.

I keep her image engraved into my mind. Using it as the motivation to get the fuck out of here. If I don't respond to Gregor, he will be a fool and attack. If something happens to her because of me, I'll never forgive myself.

Standing up to stretch, I notice a parchment lying on the floor before the door. I pick it up and read:

"Rowland Kawthorne is sentenced to the Trial of Treason. The trial will start at daybreak when the Black Sun is at its highest peak. By order of Emperor Santana, Ruler of the Hollow Realm."

I rip the paper until it makes sprinkles of white on the hard floor.

A guard enters the cell, grabbing me, and escorts me back to the throne room. Just before we enter, I seize an opportunity for an escape attempt. Looking at my loosely bound hands, I frantically searched for a weapon of some sort; some rubble from a hole in the stone where a candle was mounted appeared to be a perfect option. I need to deliver a fatal or wounding blow for my plan to succeed. I grip a fallen stone and quickly hit the guard across the head. Fleeing for freedom.

"Where do you think you are going, little man?" Calashite snarls.

"I am looking for a chamber pot. Is this not the way?" I lie. But the scowl on his beastly face says he doesn't believe me.

"There is nowhere to run, little humans. Nowhere to hide that the emperor will not find you."

"Has anyone told you how ugly you are?" With an angered growl, Calashite locks me in iron chains.

"You guys really need to make up your mind. You've changed my bindings more than a woman changes clothes." He ignored me but I thought it was funny.

"Welcome back, Rowland. How did you sleep? Is your room getting enough air?" I ignore his attempts at conversation. "You must think you are so smart. I should kill you right now for the stunt you pulled. But I already sent out all the invites. Your trial begins soon. You may choose one weapon to defend yourself with." Calashite approaches me with three items.

"If I am to die, why give me a weapon to defend myself with?"

"Rowland, you do not see the point. My subjects enjoy entertainment from time to time. It has been a little since our last trial. You should be grateful I am allowing you a weapon at all. A little beast told me you are very skilled in combat."

"How am I to choose if I am unaware of what this trial entails?"

A smile comes across Santana's face.

"I am glad you asked. The trial is whatever I deem it to be. Now, choose mace, sword, or ax?"

Strange man, in a strange land. He appears all talk. "The sword." It's the best choice because I am most skilled in it.

"Excellent. Now, take him to the arena. My audience has been waiting long enough. I want them to see what happens to traitors and escapees."

Down a widening corridor opposite the direction of my prison is lightly guarded. A grand archway leads into an open arena. I expected to see a brightened outside world versus the blood-red sky with a darkened Black Sun. It was unlike anything I've ever seen. There is a crack in the ground where black soot and toxic fumes seep from every few minutes, burning my chest and making me cough.

There is a circle of seats meant for a large crowd. A weighted ledge with one throne is placed at the center of the arena above the entryway. A crowd has already made their way to watch the trial unfold. Many beings observe in silence. My eyes caught a woman with blue skin and pointed ears staring. The crowd rises to their feet just as the emperor takes his place.

"Let the trial begin." A loud beating of the drums echoes in my head. I looked urgently around to see where my assailant would come from. The ground beneath me quakes as it shifts its form. I stand in the center of a small piece of rock with a floor of lava all around me. Ahead of me are three small islands that lead to an exit.

Part Two: Ice

Chapter Sixteen

Kaleigh

I remember feeling a cool breeze blowing through an open window, gracefully touching my long brown hair as I stood in my white silk nightgown, admiring the White Sun's beauty and thinking of a way to get to him. It has been one month to the day since Rowland was taken in the middle of the night by a dark shadow, and now he's in The Hollow Realm, a place full of unknown and immeasurable evil. One lonely prisoner hides the secrets of this realm to bargain for his release. With the dressing of my robe, I attempt to visit the prisoner once again. Greeted by two royal guards, I convince them to let me pass by offering them a barrel of ale. Down the hall lies the holding cell of the last Red Griffin bandit. I cautiously approach the bars. "My, my, aren't you looking all pretty in your nightclothes," the bandit taunts me as he lifts his hanging head with a crooked little smile.

"I'll find out how to get there," I reply determinedly.

"Night after night, you come and ask me the same questions." Heightening his voice to mock me, "How do I get there? Who are you working for?" He licks his cracked lips before continuing."But you know what, princess? You have nothing to offer me for my secrets."

Crossing my arms and turning to leave, I change my mind. "I can offer you freedom," I say over my shoulder. This is something I never offered him. At this point, I'm getting desperate. Father has already received threats from King Gregor if he doesn't get proof that his brother is alive. Last I recall we only have a couple of White Suns left in the countdown to invasion.

"The king already screwed me over once. I don't believe you." He spits at my feet.

"Well, you are just going to trust me. Because there is one thing you don't know about me."

"What's that?"

"I am not my father."

My serious nature makes him chuckle.

"All right, I'll bite. What are you planning?"

"Once you're freed, you will take me there."

"How do you know I will keep my end of the deal? I might just kill you and escape on my own."

"I have my own ways of making you submit. I will be back in two days. Be ready, bandit."

"The name's Zeke, by the way."

I quickly exit the dungeon, passing by the drunk guards. I make my way out to the Willow Well to think. While running my fingers through the water, it shifts just like before. Hoping to see Rowland again, my heart cinches at the sight of Verglas.

"Princess, it is truly wonderful to see you again." My brow furrows at the reflection speaking. "Turn around, young one."

I do as I'm told and am happy to see my grand friend gracing my presence. Running with arms open wide, I hug the dragon's massive head. Tears roll down my face.

"Dry your tears, Kaleigh. You must be strong, for the journey ahead will not be easy." Stepping back, I wipe my wet cheeks with my sleeve.

"You know what happened, don't you? Why can't I reach him? Night after night I close my eyes and think of him. Using our past encounters to bring him to life in front of me."

"You're connection isn't strong enough yet. "

"But I thought after we...um...?"

"Although you and Rowland have shared intimacy, it is only physical in nature. You two must come together in your souls. Then and only then will you be able to reach each other beyond time and space." I ponder that for a moment while she continues."Rowland is being held at the Fortress of Mal Mot. The dictator Emperor Santana has sentenced him to the Trial of Treason."

"I thought he was in the Hollow Realm. What does this trial mean? And who is this man? How do you know all of this?"

"My time with Rowland left a mark on me. A dragon bonds with its' rider. When Azula comes of age, you two will be able to communicate just as I can with Rowland. It's more difficult when he's a world away but, none the less, he is alive and that's what's important." She says with a smile.

"Can you teach me?" I asked eagerly. If I'm able to see and feel him, then I'll know how to help him.

"This is something that I cannot do. You two must figure it out on your own." A brief pause between us gave me time to think. "Do not freight my Princess. You will know what to do. And when it happens. Truly.

You both will feel and see it."

"What happens if I fail?"

"This world will be destroyed. The war between kings will end in blood." At least she is honest. "I believe you will succeed; it is written."

"He didn't get his message to his brother. How can I ensure they will not invade while I am gone?"

"It is already taken care of. Need not worry about things you cannot control. Now, I must be on my way." Verglas took to the sky, masking her image just above the castle.

Making my way out of the Willow Well Garden, I overhear whispers. Quietly, I peek around the corner and see my mother and Sir Palmer talking quietly. What are those two talking about?

Mother appears jittery. I've never seen her so unregal. "She cannot be allowed to go to that place. You know what will happen if she does."

"You must tell her the truth, my Queen." The truth about what?

"If I tell her, the king will have me killed for breaking our most sacred vow." What did you do, Mother?

"If you do not tell her and she finds out on her own, she may be the one to kill you. You know how spirited she is." Of course, I'd never actually kill her. Yell at her and never forgive her, yes, but kill? Only for Abbygale would I ever consider murdering my parents. I don't realize how close the tip of my boot is to rubble until it's echoing off the walls.

"We will continue this discussion later." Mother goes in the opposite direction from my uncle. I wait and follow her down the hall.

We pass all the bedroom quarters until coming to a halt. What are you doing, Mother? Reaching forward, Anilla presses the snout of the statue of Horace. A hidden passage is revealed as the statue is raised. The queen looks around before entering. I quickly follow, ensuring not to be seen or heard.

The stairwell is made of stone, which leads to a hidden room. I hide behind a bookshelf while watching my mother from afar. She picks up a black and gold jewelry box, opens it, and takes out a key with a pentagram at the end. The center of that pentagram is a small black stone. The Queen approached a barren wall and recited a language I had never heard.

"Yon pot sekrekache spa plus!" Out of nowhere, a steel door appeared before her. She inserts the key and turns the lock. The door opens to a dark hall. As mother enters, she quickly disappears. I slide to the floor processing what I witnessed. Angrily, I remain in my position until she returns.

As time passes, I fall asleep, only to be awakened by a loud sound from above. "Mother?" I quickly get up and make my way back up the stairs but I don't see her. "Fuck." How did she get past me without seeing me?

Desperately searching for a way out, I notice a quaint picture of a horse sticking out and press on it. The passage opens, and I wistfully exit.

I enter my room to dress for the day. A knock on my door makes me rush to change my clothes.

"Just a minute," I exclaim.

"Kaleigh? Are you still in bed?" Relieved to know it was just my sister, I opened the door. Abby raised an eyebrow in question at my disheveled appearance.

"Did you have a rough night?" Abby asked while I began brushing the hair out of my face and continuing to get dressed.

I tucked my blouse into my pants while looking in the looking glass. There were dark circles and puffiness underneath my eyes. "Oh, no. Not really. How about you?"

"No. So you gonna tell me your plan?" Abby asks while lying down on my bed.

"What do you mean?"

"Come on, Kaleigh, I know you have been down to see that bandit every night since Rowland was taken." I stop halfway through braiding my hair and look at her through my reflection.

"Abby, if we don't find him, our people will suffer from a war we cannot afford."

"Is that the only reason?" She approached me. Taking my hair and finishing the last of the tail end. "I know things sparked between you and him. It's okay to have feelings for him."

"I don't know what I feel," I respond, slightly lying. "Come now, we must see Mother and Father for breakfast." Avoiding that conversation isn't the best idea I've ever had but there is too much at stake to allow these feelings to consume me. My decisions shouldn't be influenced by him and a prophecy the dragons claim to be true.

Sitting at the head of the grand table is Father, while sitting to his right is as per her usual, Mother. Abby has always sat next to the Queen while I take my place across from them.

How did she make it back without us seeing each other?

"Kaleigh darling, how did you sleep?"

Breaking my scornful stare at my mother, I turned to answer my father, "Very well, thank you. How did you and Mother sleep?" I try to entice her. A movement or expression to make her think I know what she was actually doing last night. Well, half of what she was up to. Now that I think about it, I should've followed her through that portal.

"We slept rather well. Right, dear?" He looked at his wife.

"Yes," the Queen lies perfectly through her pearly white smile. "When is the trial for the prisoner to start?" Deflecting. That's my tactic.

"In three days. I must send an urgent word to King Gregor before this war begins," Father answers after washing down the breakfast sausage.

"Father, have you thought more about the rescue mission?" Abbygale asks. I kick my sister underneath the table for asking. She rolls her eyes at me.

"I cannot spare anyone until I know that wretched brother of his will not invade."

"I don't think it's wise of you to speak ill of my future brother-in-law." I spit out before realizing what I'd done. "If you wait any longer, myfiancé will be dead, and preventing this war, well, it may be too late for that." I raise my tone."You don't want to go down as the king who killed his people, do you?"

The room was so silent, I could hear a feather drop.

My parents scoff at me before Father says, "The decision is final. The rescue will have to wait."

I slam my hands on the table, the outburst causing the servants to jump. "You're a fool!"

Entering my room, I scream into my pillow and lie

down. Abby enters just behind me, lying beside me, and brushes my hair behind my ears. "I will be there for you when you are ready."

This is what we used to do as children. Crawl into bed, face to face, and just be each other's shoulder to cry on or strength to lean on. "I know." I sit up, "Abby, I am going to do something that you cannot be a part of, or Tristian."

Abby excitedly stands up. "I knew it! You are going to break him out, aren't you? We are coming with you."

"Don't you remember the last time you came with me? You both almost died."

"So," she shrugs her shoulders, "we are stronger together, and you know it."I walk to my balcony, debating whether to reveal what I know. She comes up beside me.

"I'm going to tell you something because you're my sister and have the right to know." I wait only for a moment to rethink what I'm about to say for fear of what it may change between us and them. "Mother has betrayed us."

"What do you mean? How could you say something like that?"

I turn to look at my sister and approach her before speaking. "I don't know how or why, but I know in my gut she betrayed us. I will find the underlying cause of it. But for now, I need to get Rowland back."

Abby stands in disbelief, but not questioning me, though. Always trusting her big sister.

She grabs my hand and asks, "What's the plan?"

"You and Tristian prepare the weapons and meet me at the statue of Horace tonight."

"Why there?"

"You will see tonight. Don't get caught, and make sure you are not seen." We hug, wish each other good luck, and devise a plan to break Zeke out of jail.

Day becomes night, the White Sun is high in the sky, and I'm on the move. Carrying a barrel of ale just like before, the guards greet me with smiles.

"Join us for a drink, Princess?"

"I'd be glad to. It must be exhausting watching a prisoner day in and day out."

The guards turned their backs while I doused their glasses in invisible sleep powder—derived from the somnum root within the Elkon Forest. Healers typically use this when their patients are in great pain. When one of the guards asked if anything was the matter, I quickly reassured him that everything was fine, and we all raised our glasses for a toast. After a few minutes of chatter, the guards fell fast asleep.

I grabbed the keys off the wall and went to Zeke's cell. As he looked up, un-waived by my presence, he smiled his crooked smile. "I have no answer–" He stopped mid-sentence as I unlocked the cell door."You are early."

I pull out the rope to bind his wrists before unlocking the ankle chains. Then proceeded to blindfold and gag him. Through muffled words, Zeke tries to protest. My blade pokes his back before delivering a threat.

"You will make no noise and will not try to resist. If you do, I will kill you before you take one step out of this world. Shake your head if you understand?"

With a nod of acknowledgment, I navigated us out of the dungeon and into the corridor. Making our way to Horace was suspenseful with every changing of the guard. I was having to hide not only myself but also Zeke. Just as I was about to turn to head toward the statue, a voice from behind called my name.

"Princess, is that you?" Roselia's soft voice came from the shadows. I hid Zeke behind the column before making my presence known.

"Roselia, good evening. I was just on my way to speak with Mother."

"Is everything okay?" she asked hesitantly.

"Yes, it is late. You should head to bed." Roselia complied with a bow and bid me goodnight. Once she was out of sight, I grabbed Zeke and went to Horace. Tristian and Abbygale were kissing when I walked up to them.

"Excuse me!" Startled, both blushed from embarrassment."Is this going to be a problem?"

"No, not at all," Abby replied.

"What is he doing here?" Tristian asked, pointing at Zeke. I guess Abby was too busy snogging her boyfriend to fill him in on everything.

"He has been to the Hollow Realm before. We need him for guidance. Nothing more."

"How are we getting there?" Tristian asked.

"You'll see." I press the snout of Horace, and he rises just like before. Abby and Tristian both look up in amazement. Walking down the spiraling steps, I looked to ensure Mother did not make it here first.

"Kaleigh, how did you know about this place?" Abby asks while looking at all the artifacts on the table, particularly interested in a parchment with a sword drawing on it. The hilt was pure gold, and the center was a blue stone. The blade was made of silver. Her eyes gazed upon it in amazement.

"Remember what I told you about Mother?" Abby turned and looked at me. "This is her secret. Somehow, she summons a portal to another world. I just need to find the key." Shuffling through things, looking for the jewelry box, I find it. Opening it, the key is perfectly placed, as though untouched.

How did this make it back? I don't understand any of this.

"How do you know this is going to work? How do you know it leads to there?" Tristian asked while holding onto Zeke's arm.

"Just before she came down here. I overheard a conversation with Sir Palmer. They were talking like they knew about this place and didn't want me to find out about it." I stated while trying to find the door.

"How would Mother know about it? Why would she keep it hidden from Father?" Abby asked still looking at the scattered parchments.

"That is what we are going to find out." I hold the key up just like Mother did.

"Is that it?" Abby asked.

"This is the key she used. But she also said some words in a language I did not understand. Look around for a parchment with a spell on it."

"A spell? Mother isn't a mage, Kaleigh. Are you sure?"

"Yes, I saw and heard everything. Just start looking–"

"I don't think we need to," Tristian interrupted. "Look."

I turned and saw the door appearing just as before.

"Is everyone ready?" With joined hands, all of us

enter through the door. The hall was a spiraling ray of emeralds, rubies, and garnet It circled all around us until we made it out on the other side.

The air was hot and dry, with a smell of ash that made us cough.

"Is everyone all right?" I asked, trying to catch my breath. Looking around, Tristian and Abby gave me a thumbs up, but Zeke was nowhere to be seen.

"Where is he? Where is Zeke?" Frantically looking for any sign of him, there were found.

Abby looked at me and asked, "What do we do now? He was supposed to be our guide."

"I don't know."

Chapter Seventeen

Rowland

I feel sweat forming on my forehead as I look around at the hateful crowd yelling insults at me. My widened eyes gaze upon the thousands and connect again with the blue woman. The heightened sound of the emperor's voice breaks my concentration, and the crowd settles down.

"On this day, justice will be served. Rowland Kawthorne of Zoldir has been charged with treason. He is sentenced to death. The trial will begin at the sound of the gong."

With a wave of his hand, the gong sounded and echoed throughout. Focusing on the task in front of me, I get the eerie feeling the island is sinking into the fires below. Searching for a way to get to the next island, I quickly realize this trial does not require a weapon. I take a quick leap of faith by throwing the sword to the ground.

As my body hits the island's edge, the breath within me gets knocked out. I cling on for life while my feet feel the burning temperatures from below. Panic swells in my chest with every beat of my heart; this piece of land sinks. I dig my fingers into the stone; mustering up the strength to pull up. Without stopping to catch my breath, I jump to the next island.

These gaps get further apart the farther I go.

I look behind me and see only lava. I turn my attention to the last jump, take a deep breath, and take my first step, but the shaking ground throws me off balance. I think of *her* as I leap above the fires below. I land with a grunt and feel a cracking sensation in my ankle. I roll to the ground, wincing in pain, unsure if it's broken or sprained. I strain to stand, turn to the emperor, and say, "Was that quick enough for you?"

The arena floor moves again, and larger walls made of rock form into shape. Each wall is ten feet high and connects at each corner. Santana smiles and says, "We will see how quickly you are." The arena falls silent as I gaze at the new task ahead. An opening marks the entrance to a vast maze. With each passing minute, the temperature rises and my knees buckle. Obstacles block my way at every turn, and a fatal blow could mean instant death.

"The trial is not finished, Rowland. You must make it through the Hell Maze to be declared victorious."

"Hell Maze? You couldn't think of a better name?" I shouted back at him.

Stepping toward the opening, I am quickly reminded of my injured foot. *Must fight through the pain.* Immediately upon entering, I'm met with a choice. I must decide between three different paths. Closing my eyes to clear my mind, I envision Verglas for an answer. *Trust in yourself.* Listening to her wisdom, I steadily move forward but drop instantly to the ground as a large metal guillotine attempts to chop me in half.

Rolling back to the entrances I attempt the path to

the right. At first, nothing appears to kill me, but I get caught between two large spikes coming out from opposite sides of the wall. Screaming as my sides are grazed by the pointed edges. Blood seeped into my already torn clothes. Once retracted, I limp back to the safety of the entrance. *Think Rowland.* He rigged all the paths with some device. We know two of three. Just need to decide the easiest path to take.

Holding my bleeding sides, blood soaking my shirt and pants, I hesitantly move to the path on the left. Cautiously awaiting the next attack, I limp through every twist and turn, keeping on my toes and ready to take action. When I see the end–marked with a sign that's labeled as such–I sigh only a little to release some of the tension in my body. The next path ahead has many twists and turns, blinding the finish line once more. My already thundering heart beats even faster as the first two turns are met with no resistance.

I've never been more anxious in my life.

Turning around the corner, a widened gap with a slim walkway is in front of me. Peeking down below, expecting to see the previous fires, I was shocked to see something far more deadly. With black skin and a pattern of red diamonds. An enlarged head with no eyes and fangs the size of a skinning knife. Slithering in a circle below, the large creature hisses, sniffing the air full of my scent from above.

"First a fucking polar bear now a death noodle! Fuck! That's a really big fucking snake."

Walking across the small bridge, I take it slow enough to maintain my balance. One slip and I'll be dinner for the beast. Unbeknownst to me, the blood from my shirt drips onto the creature below. I quickly step off at the last step and land on the next narrow pathway leading to what I hope is the last platform.

Not wanting to fret about the danger behind me, I make a run for it. The loud hissing sound makes me turn my head. I see the massive creature following me through my peripherals. Making it to the end, I turn to face the beast. It stops, its long black tongue releasing every few seconds.

"What's the matter, beast? Thought you were going to eat me?" With a loud hiss, it opens its wide mouth, spitting at me. I quickly dodge as the vile spit hits the ground; it dissipates the earth. "That's disgusting."

"You're a fool, young Lord. You shouldn't have thrown that sword away." Santana taunts me.

It lunges forward but I move out of the way. I can hear the rock cracking as its' long fang gets caught. I look around for a weapon of some sort to kill it with but can't find a dammed thing. My back hits the wall where the maze ends and the beast rears its head back once more. I close my eyes tight and envision my beautiful bride once more before death claims me.

The loud ringing of the gong sounds. I open my eyes in time to see the beast quickly slither back down to its pit. Two guards make their way to me, bind my hands in chains, and escort me out. Limping my way down the corridor, we are stopped by the emperor.

"You performed well out there, Rowland of Zoldir." By the look of his gritted teeth, I knew it was difficult for him to compliment me.

I stagger my way over to him. Smiling at my victory from today and say, "When your little game is over, just know the end of my blade will be covered in your blackened blood." With a punch to my gut, I double over with a grunt.

Grasping the back of my neck with a threatening tone, he says, "You will be dead long before you ever get the chance. Get this scum out of my sight!"

Standing in front of my cell again, Calashite unbinds my hands and pushes me through the door.

"Come on, do you have to be so rough?" I taunt a response. "Is it because I called you ugly?" A snorted sound comes from the unamused beast. My entire body aches.

Sitting on my makeshift bed, he takes my right boot off to examine my ankle. Swollen and bruised, he presses on it to ensure it is not broken. Cursing from the pain, he examines my other foot for any injuries. Plopping down, my weary hand rests upon my pounding head. I lean my head against the side wall, not moving when my guard enters with the woman from the crowd.

"Our healer will assess your injuries. Any attempt to harm her or escape will be fatal," Calashite warns.

Long green hair flows down to her waist, gracefully complimenting her pointed ears. A red garment covers her chest, short enough to expose her black-skinned stomach. Her red skirt covers her waist down to her ankles, with a slit on both sides high enough to expose the silver tattoos along her legs. Calm purple eyes examine me patiently, reaching into a brown satchel for herbs.

"I saw you." I wait for a response. "You were watching me today." The pain pulsates from my ankle as she presses down on it. The sound of laughter comes from the guards standing outside.

"Remove your shirt," she orders me with a dialect I have never heard of.

"Where are you from?" she ignores me yet again. "If you are going to be poking and prodding me, I at least need to know your name." Silence yet again as she examines my back.

"Leshana," she answers while pressing on the gashes across my back. There was pain initially, but relief followed.

"Leshana, I am Rowland. If the Emperor wants me dead, why are you tending to me?" Ignoring me once again, she continues her work. I grab her wrist, forcing her to look at me. "You should not fear me. I am not this criminal your ruler makes me out to be. I was never here until he sent his shadow beast after me."

"Drakere," she responds.

"Yes. Do you know how to speak in sentences?" A look of disdain comes across her face. "All right, I meant no offense." I lay down to relax after wrapping herbs on my ankle and other injuries. As she was packing her bag, a cloth roll coincidently rolled beside me. This allowed Leshana the chance to whisper into my ear covertly.

"I am Leshana de Dalaria," she said before Calashite entered and grabbed her by the arm.

"Times up." As they were leaving, I heard the fading words of Calashite, "The Emperor requested your presence in his bed chambers…"

I would give anything to be back in that bear's cave. At least I was free there. "Rowland, where are you?" I gaze upon Gregor who appears distraught. "I cannot do this without your guidance. Great Kings, hear my prayers, return him to me." I try to reach out to him, but his image fades. Darkness turns into light as I find myself at the center of a deadly battlefield. Lifeless bodies lay on the blood-soaked ground.

The loud sound of dragon wings fills the air above the clouds.

"Verglas, is that you?" Flames come right at me. Dodging out of the way, I glimpse a green dragon with black horns and red eyes. A rider sits upon its back, too far away to see who. Running away to seek shelter, not paying attention to my path ahead, I trip over a rock, falling onto a corpse.

It looks like her. The beautiful braids she always wears, her grip tightly on Shadow Striker. Only her face is coated in blood and soot. Those dark blue eyes that used to be bright with life are now soulless. "Kaleigh? No, no."

I cradle her in my arms and that's when I see them. Our entire group, dead on the ground.

"Good morning, beautiful." Calashite grips me by the collar, and slams me against the wall. "You know, maybe you woke up on the wrong side of the haystack."

"Shut up, scum. When you die, I will feast on your meat and use your tiny little bones as toothpicks." He snarls.

"I really think you just need to wash that foul smell out of your breath first." Back in the throne room again, it was the same setup as before, only this time there are two weapons laid out. I examine them carefully, remembering what happened yesterday.

"We do not have all the time in the world to wait for your decision," Santana states impatiently.

"If you intend on slaughtering me, what does it matter?"

"As I explained before, my subjects enjoy a show. Yesterday, you were brilliant. Many of my other prisoners didn't pass the fire stones."

"I see. You are not respected, only feared. If they only knew the truth. Just wait; when I don't die, all those followers will turn to you because they will realize what a pathetic little man you really are." Santana snaps his fingers. A moment later, a man is dragged into the room.

"You seem to have the illusion that I won't kill. So, I'll give a choice Rowland."

Santana gets to his feet, and Calashite brings him an ax. "Fight this boy in the arena today and kill him. Or…" He lines the curved blade to the boy's neck. The young man doesn't appear afraid. It's as if he's accepted his death. "I take his head off right here, right now. You have five seconds."

I don't speak, calling his bluff. "Five, four, three…"

Santana raises the ax but I still don't budge. "…two, one." I'll never forget the sound it made cutting through bone and skin as I watched the boy's head roll completely off his shoulders. His body fell forward, and a pool of blood formed around him.

I went numb after that.

"I can swing the ax if I must. Let that be a lesson for you. If the trials do not kill you, I will." I wanted to punch the smug look off his face. "You will surely die this time. The sooner you accept defeat, the sooner you won't have to endure this torture."

"This is what I live for. Plus, your healer worked some magic because I felt nothing but rage for you. And the thought of running my sword through you motivates me further."

"Get him out of my sight before I kill him." I laugh with delight.

Calashite escorts me to the arena, releases me, and hands me a mace. I refuse to step forward but am knocked to the ground in front. The metallic bars close as I stare down the horrid face of Calashite. I am going to kill that beast someday.

Picking up my mace, I await the dreadful sound of the gong. The arena is filled once again with the loyalists from before. Scanning for the one friendly person, I make eye contact with her. Leshana looks desperately at me. Watching with fear in her eyes. The settling sound of the crowd tells me that Santana has made his appearance.

"The second part of the trial is about to begin. This will be a fight to the death. Rowland of Zoldir, you will fight against,"—a pause fills me with anxiety— "Calashite the Terrible." A large square platform rises from the ground.

Two guards force me onto it. The beastly image of Calashite approaches me. All right, I fought a bear and won to fight this thing and win. I position into a fighting stance. The platform quivers with each heavy step Calashite takes.

"I told you I would feast on you when you are dead. Now I get the pleasure of killing you myself."

"Oh, come on, don't you have anything better than that?" I teased. Calashite charges forward but is knocked to the ground by a hidden force field.

"I did not say begin. Try that again, and I will make you take his place." Calashite kneels before saying, "Forgive me, Master."

"Rise, Calashite. When the gong sounds, you may proceed." He does as ordered. The ringing of the gong fuels me with a certain energy I have not felt before.

Calashite drew his sword, the fire in his eyes burning in the daylight. "I told you I would make your bones for toothpicks."

I raised my mace. "How many times are you going to say that?"

Calashite snorted a harsh, humorless sound. "As many times as I want." Calashite stepped toward me, with his sword raised high. "Do you fear the god of death, boy? You escaped him twice. It won't happen again."

From the corner of my eye, something shifted in the crowd. Like a fish breaching the sea, the crowd split in two. Something was stirring them. And I feared what it could be.

Do not get distracted.

Calashite looked, his eyes scanning the dispersing crowd. "I'm going to kill you."

I tightened the pommel of my mace and began circling the General of the Beast. "Are we going to dance or what?"

With a growl, Calashite lunged.

I jumped back, swinging my mace to block the blow he aimed for my head. I needed to kill him immediately but his armor seemed impenetrable. Calashite landed four strikes on the mace before he ducked the fifth and smashed into him. I flounced his foot, and Calashite staggered back. Not missing a second, Calashite pulled out a hidden dagger, slashing at my throat. I let the beast blow fall short, ripping through the fine material of my hand-me-down blouse.

Calashite stumbled forward into the iron bars of the platform behind him, snarling and hurling foul words; he was not disoriented as he dodged my attempt at the back of his neck. Vibrations moved through my arms as metal clinked with metal.

"Die already." Calashite panted above the roar of the restless crowd. "I am getting hungry."

I laughed, feigning to his left but sweeping for his unprotected neck. But he deflected my attempt with rapid movement. I felt the strength draining. Calashite landed a hard blow to my side, re-opening the stitched wound from before. Warm blood seeped down my body. "Now you die."

Get up.

Something or someone forced me to pick my mace back up, tackled Calashite to the ground, and beat the beast head in. Blood splattered on my face, the taste of iron and sweat was in my mouth, the color of red flushing my eyes. The beast was long dead.

Waves of throbbing, nauseating pain pulsed within my abdomen, and I felt like the yellow food would be the next thing to come out of my mouth. *This is it. This is how I die. Forgive me.* My entire body was trembling now. Weak and exhausted, covered in my own blood and the blood of my enemy, it cost me my life. He told me it would be over soon; whether or not that was true was irrelevant, as I gave in to the pain.

Chapter Eighteen

Kaleigh

Dry mouth was setting in as we walked down a path made of stone. The dry air, steaming from cracks in the ground, and the heated temperatures had a wearing effect on us. With nothing in sight for miles except the climbing black hills and red sky, I fear I may have doomed us all.

"Kaleigh, we have been traveling for hours. We need water," Abby complained.

"Drink mine. There is enough for the both of you to share." Reaching into my bag, I hand Tristian my filled waterskin. Scanning the area for any sign of shelter from the blistering rays of the Black Sun, I still see nothing. "We need to keep moving. Just keep watch for any sign of a shelter."

Traveling further down the path, I glimpse a small opening on the side of the mountain. I signal for Abby and Tristian to stay behind while I inspect with Shadow Striker. Entering the opening, the first thing I feel is a cool breeze. The cave appears to be abandoned, with no sign of life. I signal for the others to join.

"How are we going to find Rowland in this place? It seems to be abandoned," Tristian asks as he settles on the cool cave floor beside Abby.

"I do not know. But I think I should travel alone

from here," I state, closing the bag.

"That is out of the question!" Abby protested. "You need us. What happens if you get lost or worse, killed?"

"I will be okay. I will not travel too far. I will climb that mountain and get a better vantage point."

"I don't like it one bit. Tell her, Tristian," Abby says, gesturing to him to agree. Tristian raises his shoulders up and down, receiving a scoff from Abby. "You can sleep outside for all I care, then." Abby gets up and moves further back into the cave, away from him.

"I guess I will look for something to start a fire with then," Tristian states.

"I am going with you this time."

Climbing the mountainside was no simple task. The corners were rough and sharp; the temperature was unbearably hot. Wrapping my hands with a cloth bandage, I do my best to withstand the heat pressing against my palms. High above the ground, I can see for miles. Looking directly below, I see the distant silhouette of Tristian gathering up some black rocks for the fire pit.

"Tristian!" I yell as he looks up. He smiles and waves. Turning my back to him, I survey the rest of the area, shielding my eyes from the gleaming rays. A glistening reflection in the far-off distance catches my eye. Adjusting my line of sight, I see the very distant figure of a building. With a smile, I looked for Tristian to tell him the good news, but he was nowhere to be seen.

Not again.

Quickly, I climb down the side, knocking dirt and

debris everywhere.

"Abby, get out here. Tristian is gone again."

"What? I swear, we need to put a tracker on that boy." I kneel to examine his footsteps.

She asks after a few moments. "Did you find his trail?"

"I believe so." I pointed to a tall building.

"Wait, where did that come from?"

"I'll show you." They track Tristian's footsteps all the way to the outside of a vast stone wall. Noticing the many sentries posted high above us, I gesture for her to hide behind a boulder. "I think he is in there."

"Why are we whispering?"

"Because I don't know if this is hostile territory." Pointing to the top of the wall, "This place is heavily guarded. That means someone significant lives here or someone extremely dangerous."

"How do you know he is in there?"

"I don't. Where else could he be?" Slightly turning her head, I hear a sound coming from behind. Reaching for my bow, I spin around. A long steel blade barely touches the tip of my nose.

"My, my, how the tables have turned." Zeke.

"Zeke. Put your weapon down now." Abby rushes to point her blade at him, but he stops her by pressing the sharp edge deeper.

"I wouldn't. Your sister will be dead faster than you draw your sword," he warns.

"What are you doing here, Zeke?" I questioned.

"After our brief trip through that portal, I figured I would tell my master about you folks. But then, I thought. Maybe I should just kill you myself." That crooked smile came across his face once again. "But first, I want to have a little fun."

As he moves in closer, I notice Tristian standing high above us. I wait for the opportune moment to attack. I rear my fist back and crush my knuckles into the right side of his face, knee his groin, and with the weight of Tristian on him, Zeke was immobile.

"What are we going to do with him now?" Abby asked.

"I am not getting peed on again," Tristian protested. Zeke, bound at his ankles and wrist, lies on the ground, fear in his eyes as I approach him with his own sword.

Complemented with fine leaf-like carvings, the long blade is curved at the top, almost resembling the shape of a feather.

"Where did you get this from?" No answer comes from Zeke as he looks at the ground. "I have never seen a blade like this before. You didn't come here with it. Where did you get it from?"

"Kaleigh, you are wasting your time with him. Just leave him here," Abby insists.

"If I leave him, it will not help us. If I kill him, there will be no justice. He is going to lead me to where he got this. Aren't you?" I state as I cut the binding to his ankles and lift him onto his feet. "Zeke, if you haven't reported to your master by now, I am sure whatever punishment he has waiting for you will be far worse than anything my father has planned."

"You don't know who or what you are dealing with. My master has more power than you could comprehend." I place the blade firmly against Zeke's neck.

"I will not kill you. That would make me like you,

a miserable criminal with blind faith." I release him.

"You are just going to let him walk away? After everything he has done to us?" Abby protested.

"Yes. He is not a threat to us. Run to your master. Send him a message from me." Lifting the marvelous blade, I cut both cheeks. With a scream of pain, Zeke takes off toward the fortress.

"He will tell him of us and our position."

"The owner of this blade is from here. I intend to find out who and ask for an allegiance to free Rowland."

"You don't even know if that person is still alive. Or where they are. What if they follow the same master as Zeke?"

"Abby, Kaleigh has a pretty great instinct about these things. Maybe we shouldn't question her so much."

"We? I don't hear you saying anything except siding with her."

"Listen, trust in me, little sister. I have a good feeling that this sword was made by honorable people." Crossing her arms, Abby continues to show her doubt. "We need help. We three alone cannot breach those walls. I am certain there is someone here that will help us."

"Fine. But when I am right, you owe me."

"Tristian, somehow you knew Zeke was following us. Did you see the direction he came from?"

"I only saw him walking down the mountaintop opposite of you. He spotted you and was planning an ambush. So, I hid and waited for him to follow you."

"Do you think you can lead us there?"

"Yes." Returning to the cave, the Black Sun's

temperatures were rising. The shade within the cave helped keep us cool.

"We must wait here until it cools down again. I will never understand this place's Sun. There is no change in the sky's color. There is no white, only black." I started, as they settled down. While Tristian lay asleep, back turned toward us, Abby approached me with an intriguing question.

"Have you noticed anything different about him?"

"What do you mean?" I asked while cleaning my bow.

"I don't know. Why didn't he just come to tell me about Zeke? I was right there and could have warned you."

"You know how he can be sometimes. He probably was trying to be a hero."

"Yeah, you're probably right."

Chapter Nineteen

Rowland

I could see her. Not clear enough to know for sure if I was on death's door or not. If I'm to die, bless me with her face once more.

"Stay with us. Keep breathing." I thought it was her speaking to me. Breathing life into me. I was fading and fast. There was no strength left for me to lift my hand to touch her face. When I could no longer feel the pain, I could hear the angelic voices of prayers being said over me. The language was unfamiliar, then darkness consumed me. "Wake up. Wake up, Rowland."

Opening my weary eyes, I am confused at the sight above me. A brown ceiling held up in a triangle shape made of wood, hovers over me. Trying to sit up, a sting of pain comes from my stomach. My hand brushes over his covered wound.

I was stabbed. I should be dead.

Slowly, I sit up to gaze upon the unfamiliar surroundings. The floor is covered in a green satin rug that brushes up against the legs of my wooden bed. The linens are thick and smell of rosemary. One small table sits at his bedside, with only a glass on it. One long slit in the front marks the entrance to this room.

"Well this is an improvement from my last living quarters."

The tiny figure of Leshana enters with a smile on her face. "You are awake."

"Leshana? How did we get here? And where exactly is it?" Rushing over to me, she forcibly makes me lay back down and examines my wound. "Are you going to answer me?"

"We are in Dalaria."

"Okay. How? I mean, Calashite stabbed me. I thought for sure I was dead."

"Your friend came to me and helped me set you free."

"Kaleigh? Is she here?" The pale-featured familiar face of a criminal enters, making me reach for Leshana's blade. "Leshana, get behind me. This man is a criminal." Snatching the blade out of my hand, I become confused.

"No, he is a friend. He is the one that saved you."

"What? How?"

"No need to thank me, Rowland. While the Emperor left you for dead in the pit, I got word that you were here. So, I took it upon myself to save you. I figured it won me some points with your lad friend."

"I don't know how you escaped, but if you hurt Kaleigh or her family, I will kill you."

"I didn't escape. Your little princess, let me go."

"She would never do something like that unless—"

"Unless I knew how to save you." Zeke sat down next to the working Leshana. "We got off on the wrong foot. I would like to start over. My name is Zeke, and I am here because I made a deal with your princess."

Still in shock, anger rises. "I don't know what you are planning, but just because Leshana trusts you doesn't mean I do."

"Rowland, he helped me to save you."

"You cannot trust this man. He is a killer."

"All right, if you are so great, tell me how you are here. What happened? How did you know where to find me?" I sit up; Leshana grabs a cup and pours water inside it. "No lies."

"After you were taken, the Princess came to me night after night, begging for me to tell her what I knew. She even dressed up nicely. It was seductive. Her flimsy little nightgown and perfectly proportioned breasts make any man talk. Alas, I ignored her attempts, as Zeke continued to talk, I tried to swallow my anger.

His filthy little words. I should slit his throat for talking about her in such a dishonorable manner. Leshana could feel the tension build. She grabbed my arm to calm me.

"We went through a portal; I hadn't seen it before. Once we arrived, I ran away while the others were disoriented from the trip."

"Why did Kaleigh suspect you knew I was here?"

"Because I'm the reason you are here." I lunged forward, my fist connecting with Zeke's jaw as he grunted to the floor. Grabbing his jaw, he stands up and leaves. Leshana helped me get back up on my bed.

"You stupid fool." She hits the back of my head with her hand. "You would be dead if it weren't for him."

"Yeah, well, I wouldn't be here if it weren't for him."

"This woman, Kaleigh. Is she special to you?"

Is she special? Of course, I wouldn't tell her that she's been on my mind since the first moment she appeared to me in my dreams. That when we fucked in my bathroom, I never wanted anyone else but her. My heart and soul aches to be with her again. But I don't trust this elf enough to trust her with the truth.

"Yes, I suppose she is." I did not see the jealousy on Leshana's face as she changed the herbs on my bandage. "Thank you, Leshana, for everything."

"Rest now."

The foul smell of burnt flesh filled the air. The gushing sound of the blood-soaked grass made my stomach churn with unease. Lifeless bodies all around me, evidence of a deadly war. Crying in the distance, the sound of a dying animal makes me run. Verglas's beautiful white scales turning red with her own blood, each raspy breath getting hard to take.

"Verglas, what has happened here?"

"Why did you do it? You should have listened to her."

"What do you mean?"

"You betrayed us all." Her dying words sent a stab of pain through me.

I snapped awake, wiping the gathered sweat from my brow and sighing with relief that is was just a dream. Not the one I wanted. Night after night I want to see her. To feel her even if she was just a phantom of the real princess.

A stack of clothes lay next to my bed. Wiping my face and drinking a glass of water, I got dressed. A teal blouse with brown trousers and boots comfortably fit his body. I examined my wound, and a small scar and bruise was left to remind me of my win over Calashite.

Exiting the tent, my eyes were met with resistance from the High Sun's light. Examining my surroundings, all the tents appear to be the same in every way. Each is held together by tree logs, draped with blue cloth, and lined in two rows. The ground was made of dirt, no stone path, and a canopy of large trees was a roof for the entire colony.

"Rowland, come, you must meet Father." Leshana grabbed my hand and walked me to a larger tent. Upon entering, a large chair sat in the center front with two smaller chairs on each side. A tall, blue-skinned man with ivy hair and green eyes holds a wooden staff. His torso is exposed, revealing the many silver designs on his skin. All the men wore only trousers. The women covered themselves fully, minus their midsection.

"Good morning, Father. This is Rowland Kawthorne, the Savior."

"Welcome, Rowland the Savior. My name is Feanor de Dalaria. I am the leader of this camp."

"Hello."Standing there awkwardly, I did not know what else to do.

"My daughter has told me you are not from here. Where are you from?"

"I am from Zoldir." Many people gasped at the mention of home. Feanor stood up, approached, and walked around me as a predator does its prey. "Can I help you?"

"Are you the descendant of the Dragon King?"

"That is what my greatest grandfather was called."

"Then yes. You can help us." Walking back to his chair, he also signaled for someone to bring me one. "My people and I have been trapped from the outside world since the Dragon Wars. If you are the true descendant of the Dragon King, you can help free us."

"Okay. How? What do you mean by trapped?"

"Long ago, before the wars, there was one world,

one realm, one land. Dalarian." I knew the name sounded familiar to me.

The Book of Dalarian. I listened intently now.

"Dalarian was ruled by one king. It was like that for many centuries. There was a council that comprised representatives from each part of the land. Humans, Elves, Manticore, and Dragons. Santana poisoned the land when the betrayal happened, and barriers went up. Dalarian was no more."

"How am I supposed to help?"

"By killing Santana, all of his magic dies with him."

"How can I kill him? He must be immortal to be alive for centuries." A young woman brought a rolled-up parchment to Feanor. He handed it to me.

Opening it, a beautiful drawing of a blue stone was on it. A passage was written next to it in a language he did not understand.

"What does this say?" Surprised looks came across their faces.

"You cannot read the inscription?"

"No. I have never seen this language before." Feanor retrieves the parchment from me with despair, saying,

"Then you are not the Savior."

"I am sorry." I felt defeated. "I vow to still help you rid this world of that evil man."

"A vow to us is something that cannot be broken."

"I understand."

"Rytec is my general. You will learn our ways from him." With a respectful bow, I followed a younger soldier out of the tent.

Rytec was muscular in physique; his hair was

silver, fashioned into one signal braid. Upon his side, he wore a single blade and carried a spear.

"Rytec, how do you defend yourselves with no armor?"

"We need none. Since we cannot leave, there is no need."

"Then what are you training for? How did Leshana come and go?"

"You will know if she tells you so." Rytec led them to a clearing with a crowd lurking from behind them. Sneaking a peek at the recent visitor.

"I see you have come out to play." That slimy little voice of Zeke surged a wave of anger through me.

"What are you doing here, Zeke?"

"I am here to learn, just like you." Turning around, I grab a wooden staff and throw it at Zeke, which he catches with a smile. "This is going to be fun."

****

Kaleigh

With the cooling temperatures, we made our way out of the cave. Rough terrain and high elevation did not make the journey any easier. I could feel the air becoming harder to breathe at the height of their climb. Looking over my shoulder, I noticed Abbygale struggling to keep up but Tristian seemed unfazed. Which didn't sit right with me. He didn't train like I did. He should be just as out of breath as Abby.

Abby was right. Something is off about him. "Are you guys all right?" a signaled thumbs up encouraged me to keep moving. Reaching the top was met with much relief. Taking a swig of my water, I caught a beautiful sight. A field of dark green, colorful treetops, an arched opening made of vines, feels her with joy.

"Abby, Tristian, you will not believe this."

With heavy breathing, Abby makes it to the top, confused at my enthusiasm.

"What, more rocks?" She joked.

"No, don't you see the beautiful display of nature below?" Shaking her head, I wondered why only I could see it. Tristian reaches the top, appearing to be fine. Not a single heavy breath comes from him. "Do you see it?

"Not at all. It must be an illusion from all this heat." He responded, not meeting my eye.

"I am going down there. If you choose to stay up here, fine, but I am looking for some help." Not waiting for an answer, I turn and head down the mountain. Abby and Tristian soon follow.

At the edge of the grass line, I feel a surge of energy coming from in front of me. Reaching my hand out, it disappears as it hovers above the grass. Retracting it, I touch it to make sure it was still attached. "I believe this is much like the borders we have at home. All we need to do is walk through it."

"I still cannot see it," Abby states, searching for what I can only see.

"Trust me." I grab Abby's hand and reach with the other for Tristian. He hesitantly pauses and firmly grabs my hand. A surge of cold, like death, runs through my body. Letting go of his hand, I quickly draw back on Shadow Striker, my worst fear confirmed. "Who are you?"

"Kaleigh, what are you doing?" Abby stated from behind me.

"That isn't Tristian. You said something was wrong. When we touched, I knew it. I didn't want to believe it but that isn't him. So, what are you?" I challenged.

The imposter furrowed my best friend's brow."Kaleigh, you have known me for almost my entire life. It is me; I swear."

I didn't believe him, "Liar. Where is he? What have you done with him?"

A burst of laughter comes from him as his eyes turn black, and he speaks with a hardened voice. "Tristian is gone."

A cloud of black smoke releases itself from Tristian's mouth. His body falls to the ground, appearing to be lifeless. I stop Abby from running to him.

"Wait." The black shadow lets out a loud screeching sound, bringing pain to our ears. Blood leaks from within as we fall to the ground. Drawing my bow, I release an arrow at the dark creature. I curse, unsuccessful, as it goes right through him.

"Drake can't be harmed by your puny human weapons." I'm quick to think. To fight. I grabbed my crying sister and tried to pull her through the barrier just before it could attack.

"I don't want to die." Abby, scared, cries in my arms. Helplessly trapped, I am lost. I close her eyes and pray. *If you can hear me, please save us.*

A burst of purple flames shoots through the sky. The loud growl of a dragon brings them to my feet. The Drakere disappears, taking Tristian's lifeless body with it.

The dragon lands on the surface just a few feet from our position. A glistening body of purple scales, horns of blue, with golden eyes. I sense a familiarity. I know this dragon.

"Azula? Is that you?" the dragon lowers her head in a respectful bow. "Azula, you've grown up since our last meeting."

"Indeed, I have. Dragons can mature faster than you may think."

"Abby, this is Azula."

"Thank you for saving us."

"Us? That...that thing took off with Tristian. We have to go save him." Abby cried. Her wet face flushed and stained with blood. Her body, still trembling.

"It is called a Drakere," Azula said.

"What is it?" I asked.

"This was the first I had ever seen of it, but Mother passed down the knowledge that Drakere is a translation for shadow magic," Azula said.

"Why did it take Tristian?" Abby asked.

"I'm sorry, Princess. I do not know the answer. But Drakere can be killed with dragon fire."

"Then you should have killed it before it took off with Tristian." Abby was furious. I was too, but she could not blame Azula for something she was not at fault for.

"How do we get him back?" I asked.

"I do not know. I can attempt to track it from the skies, but I am afraid it has already disappeared."

"Abby, look at me." I cupped her crying sister's face. "I swear to you I will get him back. I swear with every fiber of my being, I will make them pay for this." Abby shook her head, and I planted a kiss on her forehead before hugging her tightly. "We should get moving. It could still come back."

Abby's demeanor changes almost instantly, and

she walks toward the barrier again. This time, she disappears right before them. Azula and I follow, emerging on the other side. We're met with a blissful aroma of flowers and a brightened blue sky.

"Abby, if you need time–" I started.

"Time for what? To cry over him some more. He isn't dead, Kaleigh, and I swear if you say he is…" The anger in her voice concerns me and before I can question further, Abby speaks again. "Just don't." She holds up her hand to stop me. "We will get him back. We will get them both back."

"We will talk about this." Abby brushes me off and walks away from me." This is going to harden her. "Azula, how did you get here?"

"Once I was born, Mother told me of your journey. When I found out you came here, I left at once."

"Okay, but how did you get here?"

"Don't you remember? Dragons can cross many barriers to many worlds if they choose to."

"I remember something. Why didn't Verglas join you?"

"Kaleigh, are you and the dragon going to talk all day or are we going to head into the forest?" Before I could answer, the sound of galloping horses came from within. We were soon surrounded by a dozen dark men with pointed ears. Each pointed their spears at us, making Azula snarl.

"Easy, Azula," I said.

"How did you find this place?" A man with long white hair jumps from his horse and approaches them.

"I saw it," I answer.

"That is not possible. Only Dalarians can see this place. You are not one of us."

"Dalarians'? Azula, do you know of this?"

"No," Azula says but is interrupted.

"The beast speaks?"

"Hey, her name is Azula, and she could eat you up if I let her," I said as she stood face-to-face with him. "Now listen, we mean you no harm. I came here searching for the owner of this blade. I am hoping to find some allies to take on this Master." I raise the blade, and they all get off their horse and kneel before her.

"Forgive us. We did not know Schallock was here."

"Schallock? Get up–" Abby suddenly stops me from speaking.

"We can use this to our advantage." She muttered under her breath for only my ears.

"Abby, I am not trying to deceive these people. They seem hostile enough."

"Yeah, well, they think you are someone of immense importance. We came here for help, so let us get some. Otherwise, Tristian was taken for nothing." I ponder what she says and agree.

"What is your name, skilled warrior?"

"I am Tailan de Dalaria."

"Rise, Tailan. I am Kaleigh. This is Abbygale and Azula. We need your help."

"Anything for Schallock."

"Right. Can you take us to your camp?"

"Camp?"

"Where you live. I would like to see it and meet the rest of your people." Tailan nods his head, and the others rise. Two offer their horse up for me and Abby to use.

"I will follow," Azula states as they soon start heading toward the archway within the trees.

Chapter Twenty

Rowland

Sweat dripping, dust in the air, I gripped my staff tightly as I blocked Zeke's hefty strikes. One wrong move and I would be in instant pain. This fight was not just about strength, but about honor and pride. The crowd of elves circled around them as the two outsiders fought in rage. Rytec smiled with glee at all the attention it was bringing them.

A stampede of galloping horses approached them. The crowd soon dissolved, but I stayed focused on Zeke.

"Murdering bastard."

"Stuck up, Prince."

"Is that the best you can do?" The struggle between us was intensifying. I aimed for Zeke's legs, knocking him over. Thinking I'd won, I was kicked to the ground, and we began wrestling on the ground.

"Rowland?" A familiar voice made us both stop, stand up, and turn to see her standing there. "What is going on? Are you trying to kill each other or hug?"

My eyes stay on Kaleigh but I didn't miss the satisfying grunt when Abby walked up to Zeke and punched him right in the face.

"That is for Tristian, you evil bastard."

Zeke charges at her, but I step between them.

"Back up before I give you a black eye to match your busted lip." Zeke walks away.

"I knew you would find me." I pull her into my embrace.

"What are you doing?" she asked.

"You don't appear to be happy to see me." She stood there with her arms crossed. "I was training with Rytec."

"Training? Really, Rowland." I wasn't sure how I pissed her off but I did. She turned around, got back on her horse, and followed Tailan into the camp.

****

Kaleigh

Dismounting from the horses, Tailan led us into a large tent at the back of the camp. Inside, the Elven leader Feanor was waiting to meet me.

"Why did you hit Rowland? I thought you'd be happy to find him alive?" Abby whispered in my ear.

"I am but if he was here this entire time training, instead of finding a way home, he's not the man I thought he was."

We ended that conversation and stopped in front of the camp leader.

"This is Princess Kaleigh. She carries the sword of Shallock." Feanor got up and examined me.

"Welcome, I am Feanor, leader of the Elves of Dalaria."

"Thank you."

"Is it true you came here with a dragon?" He asked.

"Well, not technically." Feanor bombards me with one question after the next, making answering him nearly impossible.

"Is the beast yours to command or not?"

"Azula is a free dragon."

"Do you carry the sword of Schallock?"

"What is a Shallot?" The entire tent is quiet.

Feanor appeared to be annoyed at me for not understanding who they thought I was. "Look, I came here to save Rowland so I can prevent a war back home. If this sword belongs to anyone, I would like to return it to its rightful owner. Then I will take my leave with him." Turning my back, the two posted guards block our exit. Pulling out my bow, in an assertive tone, "Tell them to stand down. I will not be taken prisoner."

"You are not a prisoner, young one. You may leave, but Rowland Kawthorne must stay."

"Did you not hear me? If he does not come back with me, my people will go to war with him."

"He is needed here."

"Why?"

"Take the sword and escort her to her friends." I protested, and as I discarded my bow for the sword, it shone. "Schallock." Everyone knelt before me.

"Get up. On your feet. Tell me what this Schallock is." Feanor lifted his head, his expression filled with fear and admiration. "I do not wish to fight. Please, tell me what I want to know."

As he rose to his feet, so did everyone else. "Schallock is a warrior of heart. It is the highest honor and position amongst our ranks. It is said, the one who wields will show great power."

"And you think that is me?"

"It is you. Bring her the parchment." I was handed a parchment with a drawing of a blue stone upon it and an inscription that reads:

"Schallock is the Savior. The Savior is Schallock.

The stone of Azrael shall bring the enemy of Schallock to death." What does this mean?

"She is Schallock the Savior." The entire tent began to cheer, which made me feel nervous. "We will celebrate your return with a feast."

Leaving the tent, I still didn't understand what just happened but at least they offered to feed us Abby stands by, waiting for me.

"What happened there?" She asked.

"I don't know exactly. They think I am their savior." This made Abby burst out in laughter.

"Come on, *savior*, our quarters are this way." She teased.

****

Rowland

I washed the dirt from my skin and redressed for the feast. *I feel like a fool. She hates me once again.* Exiting my tent, I see Kaleigh and Abby walking past me, and I catch my princess by the arm and drag her into the nearest tent. It was vacant. Thank the kings. I captured her lips the second I knew we were alone. She kissed me back harder. Her hands gripped my neck and tore my shirt.

"I thought you were dead," She whimpered as I tugged at her waistband. I winced and she stopped where her hand felt the scars on my torso. With a voice like death itself and blue fire burning in her eyes she said, "I'll kill the bastard who did this to you, I swear."

I smiled. "He's already dead."

She stood on the tips of her toes, capturing my lips as we discarded our clothes on the floor. She lay beneath me and I didn't wait to connect with her again. I plunged my cock deep inside of her—we both gasped and moaned.

"Fuck me fast, Rowland. Take me into oblivion." She moaned as I captured her nipple between my teeth. My pace was slow. I did as she begged me too. Fucking her tight cunt until she milked me dry. We lay in each other's arms for a while. It was as if we were making sure it was real.

"What happened to you?" She whispered, caressing the growing beard on my face.

I sighed, rubbing my fingers up and down her side. "I was in prison and forced to go through these hellish trials all because my ancestor saved the dragons."

"Verglas told me not to worry about you, but I couldn't stop. There wasn't anything I wasn't willing to do for you. I–" She stopped and my heart ached to hear her say it. "There is something I feel for you, Rowland. It's unlike anything I've ever felt before. If you were to die, I might die. Which is crazy because we don't know each other that well."

She giggled but then her face dropped into a frown. Something I couldn't ever let happen. I sat up, cupping her cheek and raising her eyes to mine. "If you're worried I don't feel the same way, just know I do. This may be the stupidest thing I'll ever say to you, but you need to know that your's the first and only pussy I've ever fucked."

"That is the stupidest thing you ever have said and I really didn't need to know that."

"But now you know that I was waiting for the right woman and I finally found her." She leaned forward and kissed me. Her hands slid over my shoulders before she straddled me rubbing her wet pussy over my hardening cock.

I let her take the lead as she lined my tip up with her entrance and she sunk down, riding me slow and looking at me intently. "I'll marry you for real, Rowland. I've fallen for you. Destiny or not, love at first sight or fight, fuck I need you. My heart is yours, just don't break it."

I gripped her ass. She picked up her pace, rubbing her clit as I claimed her mouth with mine. Nothing else mattered except this moment. I wanted to see it. To see our future together but flashes of fire and death kept showing and I stopped, not wanting to ruin this moment. I felt her clench down, her orgasm pulling mine along with. In my head, I hoped that my seed would bring us a child soon after the war ended.

"When is your next blood cycle?" I asked as we were cleaning up.

"If you're worried about me coming with child, there is no need. I take a tea once a month to prevent it."

"Once were married, will you stop?"

She paused dressing, put her hand to her stomach, and sighed. "I'm not sure I want children yet. Not until I know the world will be safe for them."

It was honest and that was good enough for me.

"Did Tristian not join you?" I asked as we came up on Abby.

Kaleigh and Abby looked to the ground. Tears swelled in their eyes. "He was taken." Abby quickly said as she walked away from them.

"Is he alive? By whom? Where?"

"Yes. One of those shadow creatures possessed his body." Abby is still devastated, you know. So am I. But we have a war to win and to avenge him is the only motivation she has now."

"He was a good man. We will save him. I promise you." The sound of a horn interrupted our gaze.

"We should go. Apparently, their *savior* has returned." She giggled making me chuckle.

Walking up to the feast, four long tables are draped in clothes and covered in food. The entire community is seated. At the front are Feanor, Leshana, and Tailan. Kaleigh and I are ushered to sit next to Abby and Zeke at the front.

"We welcome our new friends to join us in this celebration. Schallock has returned. Let us eat." The loudness of conversations, eating, and drinking filled the night.

"Feanor, who is Schallock?" I asked. Feanor gestures toward Kaleigh. "Why do they think you are, Schallock?"

"I have this fancy sword and read a parchment." I grow quiet. "But my mission was to rescue you and bring you back safely."

"I really think we need to stay and help free these people from Emperor Santana."

"Look, I understand you want to help, but my people are in danger, too. We can come back with an army if we have to." I did not like arguing with her. "Besides, they are in this protective bubble."

"Right."

"Az.

"*You have no right to ask me that. Pack your things.*" *Kaleigh takes off in the camp's direction. Entering her tent, she was shocked to find a still sleeping Abby. Walking over to wake her, she is completely bewildered at the sight before her.*

"Abbygale!"

The naked body of young Abby lies next to the naked body of Zeke. Abby springs up at her sister, yelling at her. Looking over at the sleeping man next to her, she screams.

"What happened?" freaking out, she hits Zeke. "Get out, get out now!" Zeke, confused, jumps out of the bed, grabs his clothes, and runs out of their tent. Abby puts her hands to her face and cries.

"Abby, did he? Did he force you?"

"No. We were drinking, and I started talking about Tristian and he comforted me and well, you know the rest."

"Why did you do this? You should have come to me."

"You have no right to chastise me. I loved him. He was my first love, and he is dead now because of you!"

"At least I didn't let some criminals deflower me." Abby grabbed a plate and threw it at me as she took off running.

I am going to kill him for taking advantage of her. Marching into Zeke's tent, she sees the half-naked man drinking water.

"You bastard!" punches him in the face as he turns to look.

Pulling out her knife, she tackles him to the ground. Placing her blade up to his neck, she has him pinned. "I should kill you for what you did to her."

"Kaleigh, what are you doing?" I come rushing in.

"He seduced my little sister into sleeping with him." I did not know what to do or so at that moment. "I should slice you in half."

"Get off of him!" Abby comes in, pushing me to the

side. *"You need to calm down. I am an adult and I can take care of myself."*

"You are sixteen and naïve, Abby. This is no way to honor Tristian's memory. Whoring yourself out to a criminal." Abby slaps her sister across the face.

"How dare you? You think you are so special, don't you? I am not the one who brought this upon everyone. Tristian is dead because of you. Orion is in danger because of you. At least Zeke knows who he is."

"We are leaving now!"

"No! You are leaving, we are staying." With tears in her eyes and anger in her heart, K leaves. Chasing after her, Kaleigh grabs her arm to stop her.

"Kaleigh, wait."

"No. She is right. I brought this upon everyone."

"She is just upset. You are sisters. You can work through this."

"Not this time." She jerked her hand away and headed toward the clearing where Azula was staying.

Walking back into Zeke's tent, I was shocked to see how close they became in just a brief time. It was time for him to find out how. 'She got over Tristian way too fast for this. Zeke has used dark magic before.'

"Hey guys, I think Kaleigh is leaving with Azula."

"Good. Who needs her here?" The disdain in her voice was unfamiliar to him. He notices a small smile come across Zeke's face as if he won a victory.

"Abby, can I speak with you alone?" She began packing a bag along with Zeke.

"What for? Anything you say to me can be said in front of my love."

"Your love? Zeke, what magic spell have you cast on her?"

"The only magic that is happening here is true love."

"Are you crazy? I know Abby is under a spell. Please, you have to snap out of this." Kaleigh comes up to her and tries to investigate her face, but he sees nothing but darkness.

"I am in love. And I am leaving."

"What? No," Kaleigh tries to stop him, but Zeke pushes him down. He gets back up, but Abby draws her sword.

"Back off. I am going back to be married. Zeke's Father has already approved our union. I am to be the new Princess of this world."

"Father? Zeke, I will have your head for this." They disappear into a cloud of smoke. Leshana comes rushing in.

"What happened?"

"Zeke took Abby and Kaleigh is gone. We are doomed."

"Shallock has not left. She is with her dragon in the clearing."

"Then there is still hope. I need to tell her what happened." They rush to find Kaleigh sitting across from Azula, talking.

"Kaleigh. We need to leave now."

"Don't you see I am talking to Azula?"

"It's Abby, she is gone." Kaleigh gets to her feet.

"What do you mean?"

"Zeke, he used dark magic to put a love spell on her. They are gone."

"Where?"

"She said something about getting married and becoming the new Princess of this world."

"Leshana, tell your father to prepare for war. I can get us through the barrier. We need to rescue my sister. Azula, can you contact Verglas and Xiong, we may need their help too." *Azula bowed her head in respect, and Leshana headed back into camp.*

"We will save her and our people. I promise you."

As the day turned into night, the Elves of Dalaria prepared for battle. Verglas makes her appear.

"Verglas, it is an honor to see you again. Thank you for coming."

"It is time for the world to be whole once again." *Feanor and the elf army marched into the clearing. All warriors were dressed in armor made of metal. Covering their bodies from head to toe. Each row held a unique weapon or shield. A mix of bows, swords, and spears brought hope into her heart.*

"It is an honor to welcome you." *A bow of respect is exchanged between them.*

"With the stone of Schallock and the stone Leshana wears, we will combine them to create a door for everyone to pass through. Just know that this battle will end in death for many of you. It is an honor to join you in purging this land from the evil tyrant Santana." *The entire army roared in cheers.*

As I and Leshana combined their stones an archway formed large enough for everyone to march through. I was amazed at the leadership I possessed. Feelings of admiration and respect overtook him as he gazed upon her.

"I, you mustn't let your feelings distract you." *Verglas's voice filled his ears. "Focus on the task ahead."*

Riding next to me on horseback, I watched as

Azula and Verglas took to the sky to get a scope of the enemy.

The march to Morte was tiresome for those who had not climbed the mountainside before. They were used to the comforts of home. This proved challenging for all except me, whose determination pushed her forward.

"We can rest for only a few, but we must keep moving. Our scouts see no army posted. If we are to keep up the surprise, we must keep moving."

"Kaleigh, remember none of these guys have been into battle before."

"Neither have we."

"Just relax. We will save her. I will kill Zeke myself if I have to."

I knew what he said was true. She calmed her nerves and waited until Feanor stated they were ready to travel.

Marching onward, they lined up just outside the stone walls. The sentries had their arrows pointed at them but were unaware of the dangers in the sky. With a burst of blue fire, the battle began.

****

Kaleigh

Blue and purple flames engulfed the walls of the fortress. Crying and screams of terror came from within the walls. The loud banging of drums came from within as the gigantic walls opened, and the army of Manticors marched toward them. Superior and force, I had never laid eyes on such a beast before. At the front of the army, dressed in shining emerald armor, the pale face of Zeke appeared.

The troops stopped mid-way. Azula and Verglas

landed between them, waiting for a signal to bring fire down upon them. I and Rowland walked toward the middle for a meeting.

"Return my sister to me and we can avoid unnecessary death."

"She is no longer your concern." Rowland held me back. Attacking from this position would give the opposition the high ground.

"You will die where you stand. Whatever magic you have used on her will die with you." I signaled for the attack to begin. The loud rain of fire fell up the armies, providing an advantage for the Elven army. As the Manitors came running at them, weapons raised high, and the formation of shields and spears awaited the brute force of the combined army.

The field is plagued with gore, blood, and bodies. Red, black, and blue are the new colors of what was once a deserted land and is now the scene of a perilous battle.

"Zeke, I have waited far too long for this." Standing strong, with the blood of her enemies upon her face, I stand ready to fight.

"I will take care of your whore sister once you're dead." The rage I felt made her attack first. Thrusting her sword at him with all her strength. "I may not kill you, but I will play with you first."

Spitting in his face, she continues to fight. A sword against sword, clashing with mere strength. Knowing Zeke was much stronger than her, she looked for an advantage. Zeke hits her sword from her hand. Now defenseless, she still does not back down.

"I will offer you an honorable death or to be my slave."

Chapter Twenty-One

Rowland

From a short distance, I turned to see where Kaleigh had gone. I watched as she stood in defeat against Zeke. Looking for a way to help her, I grabbed a bow from a dead Dalarian. Rearing it back, I aim it directly at him. One quick release comes flying at Zeke, but with a swift move of his sword, it is deflected. "Oh, look, your Prince saves you."

"I wouldn't be so sure about that." The loud growl of Azula came from behind him. "Shall I eat him now?"

Zeke, appearing unafraid, smiled with glee on his face. "I haven't lost yet."

Loud noises, like thunder, struck the skies. A shadow of a colossal beast hovered over the ground. Falling, hitting the ground with enough force to shake it, Verglas lay unconscious.

"Mother?" Azula rushed over to Verglas, a gleam of rage shown through her. Standing at fifty feet tall, a large green dragon with dark evil eyes challenged Azula where she stood. His black horns set symmetrical cat-like ears. From the top of his head down to the top of his tail, black spikes stood out. He was an ugly beast, with claws that still held the bloody white scales from Verglas between them.

"Meet Leijon, my father's dragon." I ran right up

to Zeke and placed a dagger right through his heart. "In death, she will be free." The last words Zeke spoke before falling to the ground, dead.

I rushed over to Verglas to tend to her many open wounds from a harsh battle. Her breath was raspy, her pulse was slow, and she was unresponsive.

"Verglas, you will be okay," I demanded.

"Azula, you need to heal her," Kaleigh commanded. The young dragon was during her own fight. "What are we going to do now, Rowland?"

"We go save Abby." The few remaining soldiers fled back into the citadel. Dalarians gathered their dead and prepared them for their journey. "Leshana, I am sorry for your lost warriors. We are breaching the castle and saving her sister."

"I will join you."

"No, you must stay and help your father."

"I know that place better than the emperor myself. You need me." I looked at Kaleigh and she agreed with Leshana. "We will make our way in through the secret tunnel. None of the guards know about it."

The battle was not over for us. We were determined to rescue Abby and get back home. I hoped that whatever magic Zeke used was gone.

****

Kaleigh

A hidden door marked an entrance into the sidewall of the castle. The corridor was small, only a child could fit through comfortably. On the other side was the vacant kitchen. Since the beginning of the attack, all loyalists were forced to evacuate to an unknown location.

Exiting the crawl space, they all could stretch their

constricted body.

"Where would they be keeping her?" I asked as she struggled to pull Rowland out of the tight hole.

"If she was to marry, it would be in guest quarters," Leshana answered.

"Take me." Leshana quietly led us down many halls until reaching the ones closest to the throne room. "Why did we stop?"

"Because there are too many guards," Rowland answered for the elf. "Last time I was here, the place was littered with them. A bit excessive if you asked me." The two warrior women didn't seem amused by my last statement. "We need a distraction. Any thoughts?" Leshana nodded her head. She began undressing herself. "What are you doing?"

"I am the emperor's lover. They will not suspect a thing." As she continued to undress, I looked away but felt a pain of embarrassment knowing she was here, too.

"Hello, boys. Want to have some fun?"

While Leshana's plan was put into action, I felt the urge to ask a question.

"Leshana is a beautiful, um, you know, woman elf."

"Yes, which she is," Rowland whispered, looking down the hall every few seconds.

"After all this is done and over with, you could come back. You know, after stopping your brother." Rowland looked at me for a moment, and leaned forward, gripping my chin between his thumb and forefinger before capturing my lips. I wasn't expecting him to make a move like that. My heart began to race, core clenched as electricity sparked between us. I'd

never felt anything more perfect in my life. With his soft lips upon mine, I pushed my tongue forward, begging for more. His firm grip around my waist tightened as he lifted me to straddle him. I could feel him hardening beneath me as the in-seam of my pants rubbed my clit. Our tongues mingled and moans were muffled but I didn't want it to end. Just as my fingers brushed the hot skin underneath his shirt, a scream resounded in the hall.

We broke apart. Our heavy breaths mingled in the space between, his eyes burning with hunger, most likely mimicking mine.

"I'm not coming back here. We will continue this later." I nodded in agreement before getting to my feet.

"How do you know where you are going?" I asked him after a few minutes.

"Just trust me." That was all I could do, but with Abby's life on the line, I did not want to risk it. We came upon a red wooden door and tried to enter. "It's locked."

"Abbygale, are you in there? It is Kaleigh. Please come out so we can go home." For a moment, there was no response. I knocked again, but nothing happened. A swarm of guards came from behind them, catching us both off guard. Our weapons were knocked to the floor and soon we were in iron chains.

We were escorted into the throne room, where Emperor Santana was waiting for them.

"Welcome back Rowland of Zoldir. I see you have brought a guest with you."

"Where is my sister, you evil bastard?" I shouted, running toward him but not before bellowing in pain when one of his man-beasts tackled me to the stone

floor.

"I swear, you'll die first for hurting her," Rowland shouted in my defense. I spat blood onto the floor before looking back at the front.

"Why don't you ask her yourself?" From within the hidden wall, black hair down to her shoulders complimented the pale face resembling that of Abbygale Orion. A black dress with green emeralds fit tightly against her body.

"That is not my sister," I croaked.

"What's the matter, big sis? Not innocent enough for you?" her voice was a deepened tone that matched the darkness in her eyes. "Where is my beloved? Where is Zeke?"

"He is dead. I killed him. You were supposed to be freed from whatever magic he used on you." Abbygale approaches me with her long black fingernails, looking deep into my eyes. I couldn't find any remnants of my sister. But it didn't stop me from trying to reach her. "Abby, look at me. I know you. I love you." Tears my eyes at the swelling panic in my chest and cracking of my heart.

She fisted my hair, wrapping my braid around her long arm as she pulled me to my feet."There is no magic being used on me. This is the real me. Now, because of you, I have lost two of my loves. It is only fair that I take two of yours."

I watched as she pulled a dagger from within her shadowed skirt, tossing me to the ground, she stopped in front of Rowland who was made to kneel at her feet. The tip of the blade aimed directly over his heart. "Say goodbye." She snickered before plunging it deep into him.

I screamed. "You already have. There is no one else I love more than my sister, you didn't have to kill him." My words weren't meant for her but for the man claiming to be the emperor of this world.

"No!" I jolted awake. Sweat dripping. I found myself back in the Dalarian camp. Quickly getting out of bed, I leave in a hurry to find Abby. "Abbygale? Abbygale, where are you?"

"Kaleigh, what's wrong?" turning around, my heart full of joy at the sight of my sister. "I just went to eat some breakfast."

"It was just a dream," I explained to Rowland, Abby, and Azula what had happened in her dream, except the part about me and Rowland nearly fucking. That's something I need to discuss with him because we keep doing that and as much as I love it, we are in the middle of a war.."And then you killed him."

"Ouch. I'm glad it was just a dream then." Rowland smiled and my stupid stomach fluttered. "Were there any good parts of this nightmare?"

I avoided that question with a question. "Where is Zeke?" Rowland and Abby gave each other a concerned look. "What? Tell me."

"Last night, during the feast, he disappeared and took Leshana with him," Rowland answered.

"I'm going to kill him! I swear." What if it was a prophecy? Another gift from the dead men above us? Couldn't send me something with a little more clarity could you?

Abby's hand caressed my shoulder, "Calm yourself. There will be plenty of time for that. I will send word to Mother asking for her help–"

"No. She gets fatally wounded in my vision." I

snapped.

"Fighting for freedom is honorable. She would be proud to die for such a cause."

"Verglas told me when I met her that these visions mean something. The one about meeting Rowland came true. I don't want any death, honorable or not, if I can prevent it."

"What do we do?" Rowland asked.

"I think I should be the one to meet with this Emperor."

"Are you crazy or just asking for a death wish?" Abby protested. "You cannot take on one man alone. Especially if he has this giant, evil dragon. At least take Azula."

"She is right, Kaleigh. With me there, it would be an even match." Azula said, speaking for the first time since this conversation started.

"All right, fine. Rowland, you and Abby need to stand by and wait for my signal. If we are going to take over, it needs to be different this time." Rowland agreed. I pray this plan was strategic and decisive.

Chapter Twenty-Two

Rowland

I saw the same as her, only she died in mine.

Once I got her alone, asking for a moment to speak with her, I decided to see if she saw everything I did. We took a hike out to the woods and I stopped near a large tree with a thick enough trunk we wouldn't be seen.

"What is it?"

I blinked, hesitating for a moment. There weren't words that would be strong enough to describe what I felt blooming inside me. I needed to know.

"Rowland, what's wrong?" I approached her, reaching out to tuck a stray hair behind her ear. She was radiant in the small rays of the sun. She was nearly backed into the tree trunk before I pressed my body against hers and claimed her lips. It felt just like the one in our dream, only better. Soon, her hands were pulling at my shirt and mine, palming her breast. We didn't need words. Only this moment as I claimed her. Our clothes were discarded on the forest floor, and her hand wrapped around my shaft. She pumped me from balls to tip as I prepped her pussy. I needed to taste her on my tongue.

My lips trailed over her neck, and I claimed a nipple, causing her to moan and dig her nails deep into my back. When I released it, I tasted her skin until landing on her pussy.

"Rowland, we're in the middle of a war." she moaned my name as my tongue caressed her clit.

"I'll stop if you ask me to but, fuck princess, I'm in love with you and want you for all eternity. I'm yours and if you don't want me, I'm yours to us whenever for whatever."

She was mine, and I was hers. Nothing would ever separate us now. I wouldn't let it.

I licked until she came on my tongue. When I stood to face her, she captured my lips, tasting herself while jumping to wrap her legs around my waste. I lined my tip to her soaking entrance and plunged deep into her.

"Fuck!" I didn't stop.

"Faster." She demanded, and I wouldn't let her down.

I found her clit with my finger and rubbed it until I felt her clenching down on me again. Her nails scraped along my back, and I pumped until I was nearly there. My balls drew up, and I fucked her against the bark of the tree until my seed spilled into her. When our eyes locked, visions of our future flashed through my mind.

"Did you see that?" She asked breathlessly. "What does this mean, Rowland?

"From now until eternity, we are one."

****

I carried myself with pride, knowing we would lead an army into battle. As a young boy, what I've wanted to do since then. Since being trapped behind a barrier and never being attacked, I only used his imagination.

"Rowland," Feanor approached him, "Please save

my daughter. That man has kept her since she was a little girl. When she helped you escape, I thought for sure she would be here for good, but" he paused, the sadness swelling in his misted eyes. "Zeke influenced her somehow. I do not understand why he would help you and then take her. Please save her."

"I will. Tailan and I will ensure she is returned home safely." I shook his hand in a promise.

"Father, we will finally avenge Mother." I overheard Tailan mention his mother for the first time since the meeting. When they were heading to the armory, I thought asking would be a clever idea.

"Tailan, what happened to your mother?"

"When we were younger. My Mother and sister were taken by the Drakere. Emperor Santana said it was the only way to maintain peace between our people. Mother was abused to the point of death. When Leshana came back and told us, I vowed to avenge her death."

"My Mother died when I was a baby. I understand your pain."

****

Kaleigh

I readied myself for my first flight. That was not the only thing making me nervous. Journeying into hostile territory was an elevated risk. And now, instead of worrying about my little sister and my people, I worry about him. The man came in out of nowhere and knocked me off my boots. I pray that we have more moments like the one in the woods when this is all over. Not the physical intimacy but the spiritual and conversational kind. Our bond will become stronger, and this is the day I'd never thought that would come to me. War. Love. Commitment. It was all I could do but pinch myself, thinking this would be another dream.

"Are you ready?" Azula said, interrupting my thoughts.

"Yes. I don't want this to end badly, so stay calm until told otherwise."

"I understand." I climbed onto the back of Azula. Just as I envisioned during our first meeting, the feeling of peace flowed through Azula and into me. I was grateful because her strength calmed the nerves threatening to take over.

Rowland and Tailan readied the Dalarian Army in position. I was tasked with breaking the barrier, rescuing Leshana, and negotiating with Emperor Santana.

Flying felt natural.

Although I'd imagined it differently, it was still magical. The air was dense and hot, but feeling weightless was worth it. The ground below was full of sand, with different mountains around it. Approaching the stone walls of the fortress, the sentries aimed to shoot at us. But none were as skilled as I. Pulling back, I aimed for three at a time while Azula dodged each arrow. After mine met their mark, we landed in the middle of a courtyard.

Loyalists were too frightened to approach; Azula's snarl and threatening fire had them scattered like mice. Azula's presence did not scare off a patrol of beastly soldiers. Circling us, the large man-like beast showed no fear.

"Welcome, Kaleigh." That slimy voice sent shivers down my spine, causing the hairs on my neck to rise.

"Zeke," I drew back on my bow, "I have not come

to fight, but I am not afraid to."

"You are a fool for coming here. Your beast is no match for my Master." Azula let out a growl of anger. "Tie the dragon down. Take her prisoner." Zeke ordered.

"You are an idiot, Zeke." We surrendered without fear because this was all part of our plan.

While escorted out of the courtyard, I could recognize each corridor from her vision. The throne room looked just like before: two dragon statues, one throne, and only a handful of guards.

"Kaleigh Orion, welcome. I hope Zeke didn't treat you too badly."

"Forgive me, you know me, but I do not know you."

"Come now, don't think I'm a fool. I know precisely why you are here." I gave him a scornful look. "You mean to rescue poor Leshana? You are foolish to think you can take what is rightfully mine." From the shadows behind the throne, Leshana has a large collar around her neck with a chain connected to the throne.

"Leshana. You are wrong. I negotiate with you." Leshana gave her a worried look. "I will take Leshana's place, but you must first agree to my terms."

"I don't think you can negotiate with me."

"I have knowledge that would interest you." Zeke walks up to Santana and whispers in his ears. Santana's face immediately shows signs of interest.

"What are your terms?"

"You will let Leshana leave with my dragon. And you will drop the barrier surrounding the Dalarians. You will leave them alone to live their lives in peace."

"What do I get?"

"Me." Santana left his throne and walked around her, looking her up and down. I felt nauseous by the foul smell seeping from him. From behind her, he put his hands upon her shoulders. I could feel the hairs on my neck raised with his hot breath. "Do we have an agreement?"

"Let the slave and dragon go free. And take this one to my bedroom."

****

Anxiously awaiting Kaleigh's signal, I felt an uneasy feeling come over me.

"Something has gone wrong. I just know it has."

"Calm your nerves. She is a powerful warrior." Tailan reassured me.

A cracking bang resounded around us, and we looked to the wall. Nothing happened. Then it starts again, louder and closer this time. I watched as the barrier began to crack like broken glass. Shattered pieces came down, and the image of Azula's silhouette came down from the sky. Tailan and I raced over to them. I would greet my princess with a victory kiss, but then I saw the look in her dragon's eyes.

"Leshana!" Tailan was delighted to see his sister was unharmed. I looked for Kaleigh but was confused when she was not there.

"Where is she?" Leshana released her grip on Tailan, walked up to me, and with somber eyes,

"She took my place," she answered.

"What do you mean? Why is she not with you?"

"She freed me and our people." Leshana tried to reassure, but nothing felt more wrong. She was meant to be here. Next to us in a victory circle, but she decided to be a sacrificial lamb. Not now. Not after we finally found each other.

"Stupid woman. She is going to get herself killed." I raced away from them and jumped on the bad of my horse. I kicked it into a gallop, ignoring Abby along the way. I had no time to explain my failure to her.

****

Kaleigh

I found myself locked in chains connected to a large wooden bed frame. A regal-looking room with walls full of paintings depicting Santana and his dragon Leijong. Above the bed, a large green canopy is hung with golden fringe off the sides. The room smelled of rotten food and alcohol. A large balcony hung off the side, too far away for me to reach, but an option for escape.

This was stupid. Getting our self-captured. Abby and Rowland should know something went wrong. They will be on their way soon. I just need to get out of here.

The vast bed chamber doors opened, and a smiling evil man came in.

"I hope you have made yourself comfortable, my dear." The doors closed. He grabbed a pitcher of wine and poured two glasses. "Do you like wine?" lifting the glass, he smells it. "I do. It calms my soul."

"A man like you has no soul." Walking up to me, he takes his vile tongue and licks the side of my cheek. I knees him in the groin and force my forehead into his. My head pounds but it knocks him back a few feet. I smile when he touches the blood coming from his broken nose.

"You are a feisty one, aren't you?" He gulps down both glasses of wine. I tried to think of something quick, so I could get free. "Are you looking for this?" a golden key hung from his neck. "Remember, if you break our deal, I will release Leijong on all elves."

"How do I know you kept your end of the deal?" Santana grabs me by my chains, unlocks them from the bedpost, and drags me over to the balcony. From the ledge, I can see for miles. In the far distance, the bright green forest stood out. Also, in the distance, the image of Azula was coming toward us. A roar washed over us like a wave.

"What is that?" Santana asked. I reached up and pretended I was going to kiss him long enough to distract his eyes from the approaching dragon. The intense moment gave me the opportunity to get the key from him. "Let's move this to the bed."

With a fake smile, I continued to distract him by taking his robe off, pushing him onto the bed, and I got on top. Taking the golden fringe rope used to tie the canopy back, I bind his wrist to each post.

Is he really this naive? Is it really this easy?

"You are a naughty girl." I amuse him with laughter. Using my hand, I rub his leg to his boot, grab his blade, and hit him in the head. Appearing to be unconscious, I grab the key from around his neck and release my wrists from the chains. Stopping for a moment to decide whether or not to kill him.

I should kill you where you lay. But that would make me like you. And death is too good like you.

Loud screams filled the night air. Running to the balcony, I hoped to signal Azula. Waving her hand and yelling.

"Azula!" the dragon came right up to me. "Abby, what are you doing here?" Santana came up behind me, using the golden rope to trap me once more.

"I am not done with you, you little bitch." Abby jumped onto the balcony, sword in hand.

"Release my sister or pay with your life."

"We had a deal." Santana looked up. His eyes went completely black as he spoke. "Leijong attack."

A loud, thundering sound came from the skies. An enormous beast with green scales, red eyes, and brown horns came at Azula.

"Get Kaleigh. I will manage this one." Azula growled and took off to face the evil beast. Abby blew the horn Tailan gave her but was hit from behind. Zeke was standing over her.

"Did you honestly think you could defeat him?" Abby did not answer him. She kicked his feet right from underneath him. He hit the ground hard, and with a grunt, he was surprised. Abby picked up the sword he had and took off after us.

Chapter Twenty-Three

Rowland

Striding up to the wall, I was shocked to find it open. A flood of people were evacuating. Upon entering, I learned why. Purple flames were everywhere, and in the sky, I saw Azula in the midst of her own fight with a large green dragon. Getting off my horse, I raced inside to find Kaleigh.

A large guard meets me and challenges me with their sword.

"You killed Calashite. It won't be so easy."

"Bring it on then." Our swords clashed and shields banged against one another. I didn't have time for this. We fought until I could get an advantage. Knocking the guard onto his knees, I sliced his head off. "I found that rather easy."

After continued my search for her. Starting in the throne room.

"Rowland?" the familiar voice made him turn around.

"Where is she? Have you seen her?" Abby answered, holding a small wound on her head.

"He has her. I tried to stop him, but then Zeke knocked me on my ass." Walking in from behind Abby, Zeke grabbed her.

"Remember me." Abby elbowed him without a

second thought.

I kicked his weapons from his hands and forced him to his feet, punching him until I saw blood pouring from his nose.

"Tell me where he has taken her and I will let you live as a prisoner for the rest of your miserable life." I tightened my hold on his collar. His eyes searched mine for a lie he wouldn't find.

"Home. She's back in Orion Fortress but I wouldn't go there if I were you." I narrowed my eyes at him. "You'll find nothing but death and destruction. I wouldn't be surp–"

A blade stuck out from his mouth, blood dripping from the corners and I watched as his soul left his eyes before I dropped his limp body to the floor.

I looked at Abby who shrugged, "You said you would let him live. I vowed no such thing."

"We should get going."

****

"You must know his plans for her. I mean, he is your Father." Abby's demands are heard throughout the camp. Beaten, bloody, and with a face full of cuts, the last guard hangs tied up by his arms and ankles to a wooden post.

"I already told you all I know." In his weakened state, he struggled to speak and stay conscious enough for interrogation. From the corner of the room, dressed in acceptable leather pants and a button white blouse, I watch Abbygale beat the truth out of the prisoner.

"Well, I don't believe you." Another punch across his face renders him unconscious. I grasp the young lady's wrist in a split second before she strikes again.

"Beating him to death will not help us, nor your

sister."

"If only we would have done this sooner, she would have never been taken." Wiping the blood from her hands, I sense the darkened toil this journey has had her.

"I promise we will save your sister and our kingdoms. The emperor will not win."

"Your empty promises mean nothing to me. You were foolish to trust that elf. I knew she would not be trusted when she returned and–" the tears formed in her eyes. "My sister is the most honorable woman I know. More than my own mother. I will not stay here another minute." Reaching out to her, I pull her in for an embracing hug.

"Leshana will pay for her crimes against her people. Tailan will see to her betrayal not going unpunished." With a brotherly kiss upon her head, I could feel the tension in her shoulders, relieved just a little. "Azula is preparing for us to return home as we speak."

"What are we going to do with him?" she sternly asked, pointing at the unconscious man.

"I believe Tailan will take care of both. He is no longer our problem." With the swift opening of the tent, a guard enters.

"Lord Tailan requests you to escort the prisoner to him at once." Abby and I exchange glances, and he gives the guard a nod of understanding.

With the weight of the prisoner upon my back, my mind drifts, searching for a way to connect with Kaleigh. If you can hear my prayers, Verglas, Kaleigh, Great Kings of The Past, know I am coming. Everything will be set right. Entering the tent, Tailan sits where his late Father once did, and Leshana is chained to the ground before him.

"Bring the prisoner next to her. They will face the same trial. Their charges are the same."

"Look at you, brother. Sitting where our foolish Father used to sit." Glancing over at Leshana, I see the darkness in her eyes.

"Silence! You have no right to speak of the man you murdered." A laughter of pure evil comes from her. This is not the same woman that I met so long ago. "Leshana de Dalaria you are both sentenced to death for the betrayal and murder of innocence. If anybody present wishes to speak on your behalf, they must speak now." Many of the guards and others present looked around.

"Lord Tailan," gasps and shock came across everyone's face as I spoke. "Is it possible that Leshana is under the influence of the Drakere?"

"Lord Rowland, we have performed several tests upon her, and they were all met with the same results. She decided purely of her own heart and mind." Abby shot me a disapproving look at the thought of me speaking up. "The prisoners will be executed at dawn." The crowd disperses, and the prisoners are taken back to their cells to await their execution.

I venture out to the clearing to meet with Azula. Her vibrant purple scales shine in the rays of the brightened sky. Offsetting the depressing image from far beyond the border.

"Azula, are you almost ready to head back home?" looking over at me, Azula's eyes glazed with rage.

"The answer is simple. We fly." Her tone and demeanor are unfamiliar to the soft-spoken dragon he met before.

"Are you angry with me?" a snort of anger confirms his suspicions. "Are you and Abby going to blame me for trusting someone who appeared before me in a caring manner? How did I know she was deceiving me the entire time?"

"You have the gift of sight, do you not?"

"What does that have to do with anything?"

"You are undeserving if you do not understand the power that you wield. My Mother... Mother should have never bonded with someone so undeserving of that honor." I, now confused about what Azula was saying, turned to leave to fetch Abbygale.

"Azula, I know I failed everyone, but I will make this right. Tristian will not have died for nothing. And Kaleigh will be rescued, and our kingdoms made safe again." The young dragon turned her head away in disgust at the sight of him. "I will retrieve Princess Abbygale so we can go."

Walking back into the camp, I notice the hushed voices and whispers amongst the Dalarians. As if their town gossip was about me and the recent events that had transpired. Leshana's deceit led to the capture of Kaleigh, the downfall of our kingdoms, and the potential demise of the realm. This is what Verglas has been warning me about. The visions of death and destruction are falling into place, and it is all because of me.

"Is Azula ready to get out of this hellhole?" Abby's eagerness to leave was more than about rescuing her sister. It was about avenging her lover's death. Tristian Aerogun was the kindest soul I ever met. His life was taken by the Drakere by the order of Emperor Santana.

"Yes, I believe she is." Standing in the middle of the tent, I examined the young Princess, packing her bag. An instant pounding in my head, ringing in my ears, and blurred vision knocks me to the ground. Convulsing uncontrollably, the world around me shifts from Dalaria to Orion Fortress. Screams from thousands can be heard for miles. Raging fires from above have turned this once beautiful city to ash. At the center, the once-great king lies beside his queen on the blood-soaked ground. Standing with pride in his heart, the red-soaked steel blade in hand bears my reflection.

"How could you? I trusted you!" The weeping voice of Princess Kaleigh Orion screams in despair at the sight of betrayal.

"You should've known, my dear Princess. This realm is ruled by a Kawthorne, not an Orion."

"You betrayed me. I thought…"

"You thought what? That I loved you? I was playing coy. Getting you to lead me to victory." A wicked smile sends anger through her. As she aims her last arrow right at my heart. Without a single moment of hesitation, she releases, and her world slows down all around her.

"Rowland, Rowland," the vague image of Abby standing over me brings me back to reality. "What happened?"

"I… I think I was given a vision."

"I thought those only happened in your sleep?"

"Me too. But I think because Kaleigh and I finally connected on a spiritual level, they'll be stronger and come whenever I need to see something." I got to my feet. "Abby, you must move on without me."

A stern and confused look crosses her face."What

do you mean?"

"I have a bad feeling that going back with you will only bring more death." A slap across my face leaves a sting on his cheek. "What the hell was that for?"

"You are a coward, Rowland, after everything my sister has done and lost for you. Are you just going to stay here? With people who do not even know you? You would be dead if it were not for Kaleigh. Tristian is already gone–" tears swelled in her eyes, "You are no Lord. No savior. Just a coward. I thought you would do anything for the person you love most in this world. Was I wrong?"

"Abbygale, you must understand. What I just saw cannot happen."

"Are you staying based on some vision? Are you stupid?"

"You wouldn't understand." She reached over to grip my hand. Comforting me.

"Rowland, I lost the only man I ever loved and loved me back. I see the way you two look at each other. I know what unspoken feelings are. If I show up without you. It will break her heart even more."

"Abby, I saw myself standing over the dead bodies of your mother and Father."

"You are to kill my mother and Father?" quickly, she stands up, appearing to soak in what I just said.

"In doing so, Kaleigh kills me. I do not know if it was me I saw. My eyes were not mine. My voice was not mine."

"What color were your eyes? Were they black?"

"Yes, why? Do you know what that means?"

"Drake. That happened to Tristian right before he–"

"Of course. Now it all makes sense." I excitedly get up. "Abby, we need to go right now." With a nod of agreement, they rush out to the clearing. "Azula, we must leave right away.

Part Three: War

Chapter Twenty-Four

Kaleigh

The hardened black scales of this evil dragon send waves of fear through my chained bodice. Attached to the metal saddle upon the back of Leijon is the dark dragon of Emperor Santana. A force of evil that has not roamed for centuries can now rule over the realm once more. A swift flight over the borders that protect the rest of the world from this dark power is now gone.

"Are you happy to be home, my dear?" His scratchy voice sends tremors down her spine. I would spit in your face if this cloth were not keeping my mouth from speaking. "I believe your mother will be delighted to know I have returned you safely to her. But as for your father, well, he might have to meet my dear friend here." He pats the hardened head of Leijong.

A rough landing of leaves deepened bruises upon I's chained wrist. Amid my home, the White Sun is high in the sky, and the cool breeze blows the sweat from my brow. With a tug from the leash, the emperor leads me through my solitude, the Willow Well Garden. Broken down to pieces as Leijong sets fire to it. I try to protest but am swiftly knocked unconscious by a blow to the head. "Now, we don't want you making masking noise and waking the guards, do we?"

"Kaleigh, darling, wake up." A faded image of my

mother, Queen Anilla, becomes known. With a pounding head, I sit straight up, making myself dizzy. "Slowly, my dear. Your journey home was rough. A falling brick knocked you out."

"What? No, where is he?"

"Father? He is tending to business in the throne room." Queen Anilla presses a cold cloth on her head.

"This isn't right. Where is Abby?"

"Oh dear, you don't remember, do you? That brick must've done a number on you." I am now confused. "Your dear baby sister was killed some nights ago." My heart beats with anxiety and fear.

"No, that isn't possible. Who are you?" I fight and push the Queen away. "Get away from me, you imposter."

"Kaleigh, darling, calm down. You mustn't get upset over something that happened many Suns ago." This is a vision or magic.

"Tell me something, Mother, if that is who you are, why did you name me?" I looked to see the struggle on the woman's face.

"Honestly, do you think one question will prove I am your mother? You should not need any proof. I am who I say I am." An awkward pause gives me time to reach for the hidden blade attached to the backside of her headboard. In a quick movement, I place the blade on the woman's neck. "What on earth are you doing, child?"

"You are not my mother. Who are you, and where is the emperor?" I see the reflection of an evil face on the golden plate on her bed. Eyes black as coal bearing a resemblance to the eyes of a Drakere.

"Well, he was right. You are the smarter of the

two."

"Get out of my mother before I kill you."

"You can't kill me. If I die, so does she." The possessor warns.

"I will rid you of her and kill you." I knock my mother unconscious with a swift blow to the back of her head. Taking some rope, I tie her mother's body to the chair next to the fireplace. "I will be back for you, Mother." With a kiss on my forehead, I exit my room to survey the castle.

Sneaking down the narrow corridors, I overhear a familiar voice.

"We must warn the Princess somehow." It was Sir Palmer and Roselia.

"I don't know how."

"You are her ladies' maid. The emperor has permitted you access to her quarters."

"The Queen is in there with her. And so is that thing." Staying behind the corner wall, I whistle in their direction.

"Do you hear that?" Sir Palmer is familiar with the sound. When I was a little girl, he taught her to whistle whenever she was in trouble, and he would know to get help. "Kaleigh? Is that you?" he asks in a low whisper.

"Yes," I said slightly, waving to them toward her. "What the hell happened here?"

"I'm afraid the kingdom has lost, my dear," Sir Palmer states with sadness in his voice. "Once we heard that beast destroying the garden, the king sent our armies to rescue you and take them prisoner. He didn't account for the dark magic."

"What happened to Father and the rest of our people?" Roselia looks toward the ground before speaking.

"Your Father has joined the Great Kings in the sky." The news of her father's death pained her. As tears swelled and a lump formed in her throat, she tried to hold back from crying. "I'm sorry, Your Highness."

"Roselia, Sir Palmer, what about my sister? That thing inside Mother said she is dead too."

"Your sister has yet to return," Roselia answers.

"Okay, that's good. That means we can still take back the kingdom." Glances of despair between Sir Palmer and Roselia do not share the same hope as her. "I mean, we haven't lost everyone, have we?"

"Once the barriers dropped, King Gregor and his armies marched into our lands and took over. The king struck a deal with the emperor. He would be his new general and help him take over each land within the realm."

"And Lord Rowland? I presume he knows nothing about this?"

"He has yet to return, too. What are we going to do?" asked Roselia.

"All right, I need to get into the Snow Forest. I have powerful allies there that can help. You two must gather whoever you can that is still loyal to my father. If it is a war Santana wants, it is a war he shall have."

Sneaking through the palace was no issue for me. That was one advantage I had over anyone else in this castle besides Tristian. The one person who stood by her side through everything. If you are with the Great Kings in the sky, dear friend, know I miss you more than you could understand. A widening corridor led to the armory packed with the Emperor's humanoid guards. The one thing they did not know that I did was the small hole in the wall that allowed passage between the Armory and the linen closet. The small wooden door that opened into the small closet was on the far side of the wall, connecting to the back of the armory.

Tristian and I used this to get past Sir Palmer just before heading out on a hunt her father had never approved of. I know a hole is in here somewhere. Moving all the linens to the stone floor, with one push, the bricks fell to the ground beneath her. There was a slight thud with the soft cushion blankets once they hit the ground. Squeezing through the opening, I found myself in the back, where all the archery equipment was kept.

I desperately looked for my bow, but it was nowhere to be found. The emperor must have it. That bastard has taken the last thing from me. On the back, mounted behind a glass case, was the sword of Schallock.

That stupid fool. He took my bow, but not that beautiful piece of weaponry.

With a hilt brushed with silver and gold, the sword was delicately balanced. A small piece was missing from the round placeholder at the end. It must be for the stone. Otherwise, why would the sword and stone be separated? He must have taken that, too. Exiting the Armory through the linen closet, I returned everything as it was just before. Each step I took forward was another step closer to the stables. With a flutter of adrenaline, I ran to the stables. Upon entering, I stopped to catch my breath. Where are the horses? The vacant stable did not put my worry at ease. I will walk to the Snow Forest from here. Peeking out to ensure I was not followed, a Manticore's authoritative, unfamiliar voice sent a shiver down my back.

"I swear if you let her get away, I will behead you before the Master has time to."

"She is in the stables. There is only one way in and one way out. We have the entire place surrounded." The leader snorted in doubt. He is right. I do not have a way out of here. The heavy footsteps of the guards drew closer. Glancing around, I tried to think of a hiding place, but it would be useless. They would find me, eventually.

"This is your only chance to come out unharmed. The emperor doesn't want us to kill you, but he never said not to hurt you."

"Why don't you come in and face me like the beast you appear to be!" I yelled back to her. The footsteps drew closer and faster as if my challenger was calling her bluff. Standing eight feet tall, the large man-beast swung his vast ax at me. Dodging the deadly blow, I found myself on the stable floors.

"You see, Princess, I can take you in the effortless way or the hard way. Which one do you prefer?" A loud shattering of the roof came crashing in on them.

"How about neither?" Standing during the debris, the beautiful blue scales of Verglas the Ice Dragon shined bright. "Get on my back, Kaleigh." I did as I was told. The guards were all burned to a crisp with a burst of flames.

Flying on Verglas's back was just as appealing as flying upon Azula's. The cool breeze and freedom of flying were pure. That moment did not last long. The thundering growl of Leijong came from behind us. A burst of black flames shot past them. "Hold on, this is going to get rough." The fight was not over. Leijon was fast and powerful, but Verglas was slightly quicker. Growling, scratching, biting, I struggled to hold on.

From behind, a burst of White flames knocked Leijong from the deepened grip upon Verglas. "Get away from my sister." Xiong, Verglas's brother, hit the evil dragon away from us. After the small fight between them was over, Xiong escorted us back to their home in the Ice Cave.

"You foolish girl. Why did you come back?" Xiong was scolding me for getting Verglas injured.

"It is not her fault, Xiong. Calm down, and I will heal. My wounds are not fatal."

"Verglas, I'm sorry this happened to you, but I must thank you for saving me."

"It is what is right. Azula would kill me herself if I left you to that man."

"How long has it been like this?"

"A few weeks ago, the barriers came down. King Gregor marched in, and the war between kings began."

"Weeks? But I was only in the Hollow Realm for two weeks. The barriers weren't removed until we rescued Leshana, and that was only a couple of White Suns ago."

"Time works differently in each realm, my dear. One week in the Hollow Realm is a couple of weeks in the rest of the world."

"How did the emperor convince King Gregor to ally with him?"

"Before you returned with him, he sent a messenger to secure the fortress and allegiance before arriving."

"That makes little sense, Sir Palmer said–"

"Sir Palmer is no longer your ally. He is with the

emperor. How do you think they knew you were in the stables?"

"How does one man possess the power to control everyone? I have been betrayed by those closest to me, and for what? All so one man can take over the entire world. Before all this, I did not know other species, let alone other parts of this world. First Mother, then Sir Palmer and Roselia, and now my father is dead. All because I ventured into this forsaken forest to find a man. A man that I did not know. I was a fool. I was naïve to believe I could save our people."

"You mustn't be so hard on yourself." Verglas tries to sympathize with her. "This was not what you had planned would happen, but your first vision happened months ago. Now you are here. You can stop the rest from coming true."

"Verglas, how am I supposed to overcome a man that possesses the darkest magic ever known? Please tell me if you have any ideas. Because not only did I lose my best friend and Father, but now my home."

"Princess Kaleigh, when I first met you. I tried to burn you alive. I have investigated your heart and know you can defeat this evil. With my sister and I by your side, there is nothing you cannot do."

"Wow, Xiong. If only I could believe you." With defeat, I leave the cave for a walk to clear her head.

The clean, crystalized water reflects an older, more mature woman than when she investigated this pool. "Father, if you are with the Great Kings in the sky, hear me say that I am sorry for my failure. I will do what I must to ensure our people are free again."

****

Rowland

A refreshing breeze fills the air, providing a soothing atmosphere to the surroundings. Abbygale is positioned at the front, closer to Azula's two long horns, while I sit toward the end of her tail. Thoughts of what is to race through my mind. I hope you are safe, Kaleigh. I hope our kingdoms are not at war. If they are, I pray they fight against that oppressive ruler. In the distance, a wall of falling snow, once concealed behind an obstacle, is now visible.

"I think that's the entrance to the Snow Forest," I yelled, hoping they would hear me. They ignored me, or Azula increased her speed, and the wind moved too fast within their ears. Crossing into the tundra sent spikes of ice through his exposed skin. "Can we land somewhere warm?"

"What?" Abby turned and asked.

"Can we land somewhere warm?"I rub my hands along my arms, hoping she would get the message. A thumbs up from Abby told me she passed the word to Azula. Diving deep into the snow-covered forest below, adrenaline rushed through my body. A soft landing in a small clearing gave his stomach time to settle. "I thought we were landing somewhere warmer. Azula sensed her mother's presence in her home nearby."

"We must get back to the fortress and warn your King."

"There is no need. He already knows," Azula started with a saddened voice.

"How far is your home?"

"Rowland, you do not recall where we are in these woods?" Abby teased. "I thought you would remember where we first met." Looking around, he saw what remained of the shelter he and Tristian built.

"I see." They trekked their way through the forest. After some time passed, the familiar sound of the waterfall rushed through his ears. "We are near." In a few minutes, they were standing outside the cave.

"Rowland?" a familiar voice made him turn around. "What are you doing here?" I rushed to Kaleigh and hugged her with all his might. "I'm happy to see you too, but where is my sister?"

"Turn around." Standing behind her was the smiling face of young Abbygale. They hugged each other even tighter. "It's good to see you, sis. What happened? How did you escape?"

"Why don't you all come inside where it is warm? Then I can answer all your questions." Ushering them to the inside of the cave, the warmth of the fires melted the chill from their bones.

"Azula, Rowland, and Princess Abbygale, it is good to see you." Azula runs over to her injured Mother. "I am all right, dear. Your uncle is tending to me."

"These look like dragon bites. That dark one is here, isn't he?"

"Yes, but Xiong and I took care of him." They nuzzled each other. Azula settled in next to her mother.

"Where are brother and sister?" Azula asked.

"They went out to look for more dragons with Xiong."

"There are more dragons out there? I thought you were the last of your kind?" Kaleigh asked.

"We are the last of the line of Ice Dragons. Just like the dark dragon, there are other species within our race. Since the barriers are no longer up, it is easier to search for them."

"The more firepower, the better," Abbygale commented.

As time passed, the group shared the events of the past couple of days. I recounted the events after the invasion, while Kaleigh discussed what happened on the trip home.

"So, you're telling me that one day in the Hollow Realm is like one week in our world?" Abby asked with curiosity in her eyes. "And Father, is he truly dead?"

"All I know is what I was told. I did not have time to see Father myself."

"And my fool brother sided with the emperor? He must have used his magic on him. My brother is reckless with anger, but he would never side with an evil man like Santana unless…"

"Unless he had no choice. Yes, I know."

"Drakere possesses Mother. There is no reason she would sit next to the man who killed our father."

"Abby, Mother used that portal under Horace several times. Sir Palmer and she had a secret conversation. I can't help but think she had no free will in this." A moment of silence filled the cave. The flickering embers of the fires and the shallow breaths of the injured dragons echoed through the cave. Standing tall, I prepared myself for a speech.

"All right, so this is bad, like terrible, but we have come so far. We have not lost yet. Xiong is getting more dragons to fight with us. Tailan and his armies are searching for others to join in. I am sure there is something we can do besides sitting here and letting our people suffer. Santana has already taken enough from all of us. My brother, your parents, we will stop this."

"Nice speech, but how are the three of us going to

take on a powerful man like him?'' The doubt in Abby's voice did not make his confidence waiver.

"Kaleigh, you know your way in and out of that fortress like the back of your hand, right?"

"Yes. What does that have to do with anything?"

"I bet you know how to get through there without being seen. I also bet Abby knows a few secrets of her own. Am I right?"

"I see what you're planning, but it will not work."

"Why?"

"My sister and I grew up in that fortress. But I did not know about the secret room underneath Horace. Our Mother has lived in that palace far longer than we have been alive. There are things she knows about that even I don't."

"Well, we can't just sit here until help arrives. Santana is going to make the people submit, and if they do not, they will be killed."

"We don't want our people to suffer, but we have nothing to fight with. We have three swords and two injured dragons. That is not enough to fight and win."

"Maybe we don't have to win. Maybe we must hold him off long enough for reinforcements to arrive."

"Abby, if you agree, I will only go through with this plan."

"You are both hopeless, but what else can we do? I vowed to Tristian that I would avenge him no matter what. If I die fighting, then so be it. At least when I meet him in the afterlife, I can say I gave it my all." Looking over at Verglas and Azula, I gesture for an answer.

"You already know our answer."

"All right, we will travel to each village at High

Sun and get as many loyal troops as possible to fight with us. The children need a place to stay and be looked after."

"They can come here," Verglas stated, "There is nowhere safer than a dragon's cave. No evil can cross over the Waterfall."

"Let's all get some rest for tomorrow when the actual work begins."

After an hour, Kaleigh and Abbygale were tucked in close to each other, fast asleep. The thoughts of the upcoming war kept me from falling asleep.

How could you do it, brother? How could you betray everything Father taught us? This must be about the Stones. Unable to sleep, I exit the cave to get some water.

"Rowland, is everything all right?" Kaleigh's calm voice sends a smile across my face. Turning around to face her, I stare at the beautiful figure glowing in the rays of the White Sun. She walks closer, and my stomach flips with anxiety. I want her body pressed against mine, once more. But I remember what she said last time. War. Her gaze tells me to reach out for her. The tension between us only grows stronger. In a split second, Kaleigh is in my arms, and we embrace each other with a kiss of passion that slows our surrounding world.

My heart beat fast with the newfound lust for her. With skin so fair and soft, a kiss on her neck intensifies the moment. In between our lips locking, Kaleigh says, "Rowland, Rowland, slow down." I do as I'm told and merely hold her close. "We cannot let this come in the way of our mission. We are going to war tomorrow."

"When we are victories, I'll have you pinned

beneath me screaming my name for the entire realm to hear. That I promise."

Chapter Twenty-Five

Kaleigh

Dawn was fast approaching, with the High Sun rising to its highest peak. The temperatures also increased ever so slightly. The events from the night before replayed in my mind over and over.

"So, if we walk, it will take about a day to get there."

"Who said anything about walking?" Azula and Verglas stepped out of their home. "We are well enough to travel. The sooner we get to your people, the sooner we can rid this world of the emperor."

"Verglas, are you sure?" Rowland questioned.

"I am riding with Verglas if that is all right with her." Abbygale's tone was full of hate. She wanted nothing more than to be as far away from me as possible. "And don't even think about riding with me." A scornful look toward me made her feel even more terrible about what she said.

"All right, Rowland, Kaleigh. Let's go. We haven't got all day." Azula started leaning her wing down for them to climb onto.

Up in the air, I could see an aerial view of her home, from Ice Village to the Marketplace. The air was crisp and moist. The world felt calm and at peace in the skies. Ahead of us, just a few feet, was the glistening blue figure of Verglas. Gleaming with the rays of the High Sun. Upon her back, Abbygale's flowing hair danced with the wind.

Across my waist were the two powerful arms of the man I've grown to care for. His touch was electrifying. Turning my head ever so slightly to glimpse him, the stumbled hairs upon his chin showed the mature features of a young man. Before he caught my stare, Azula swooped down to land in the middle of the village. In a vast circle, the villagers gathered around them.

"Welcome, Your Royal Highness. What may we do for you on this fine day?"A young barmaid bowed respectfully as she greeted them.

"We need the entire village to meet here. We have an important message for everyone to hear."

"Right away—"

Before she could finish. Rowland interrupted her."Katrina?"

"Rowland." An enormous smile came across my face as she ran up and hugged him as if he had just returned from war.

"Looks like you got some competition," Abby taunted in my ear.

"With a barmaid?" I chuckled.

"Did you find your cousin? How did your journey fare out the rest of the way?"

"Cousin?" I asked, butting into their conversation.

"Oh, princess, please forgive me. I didn't know he was your cousin."

"Katrina. Right, well, I am not Rowland's cousin. I'm his fiancé and it would be best if you fetched everyone as I asked you to." She looked at Rowland, then back at me, before scurrying off to do as she was told."Well played, sis. Using your title to win," Abby said.

"Oh, shut up. Like you wouldn't do the same."

Hushed murmurs and exchanged looks between the townsfolk had me feeling nauseated. I've never spoken to these people my entire life. Now I'm expected to lead them into a battle I'm not sure any of us will survive.

"Thank you all for coming. I know that the weather isn't kind now, but I will make this happen as quickly as possible." Looking over to Azula, the dragon gives a nod of encouragement. "For those of you who do not already know, our land has been invaded." Shock and awe spread through the crowd like the waves upon the shore.

"But the king, he—"

"The king is dead," Abby interrupted. "What my dear sister is saying is true. The king from the other side invaded and allied me with the dark sorcerer, who calls me an emperor."

"What about the knights? Why haven't they come to warn us? What are you doing with those beasts?" one villager asked, but before she could answer, others started speaking.

"How do we know you are not spreading lies?"

"You travel with dragons. They are evil." The crowd became unruly and hostile. "How can we be sure you are the princess? When none of us have ever laid eyes upon you?"

"Because I have seen her," the young BarMaid spoke up. "When I was a girl, the princess showed me a kindness I never forgot." I examined the woman closer.

"My childhood home caught fire in the village in Orion. Amongst many others, however, I was not as fortunate as others. My mother rushed into the flames to save me. When a roof collapsed, we were both knocked unconscious. The next thing I knew, I was lying in the infirmary with my hand being held by her. My mother did not make it. The king granted my father ownership of the Tavern so we could have a place to live." The memory of that day came flooding back to me. Tristian was not the only child who lost a parent that day. "Listen to her and trust in her like I do."

"Thank you, Katrina." I had a newfound respect for the young lady. "These beasts, as you call them, are on our side. To my right is Azula, daughter of Verglas, the great Ice Dragon. They have saved me and my companions' lives more than I can account for. You have no reason to fear." Both dragons settled down to listen to the rest of her speech. "I will not lie to you. There is evil in our land. A dark dragon, the color of emerald, bears no allegiance to these two. Alongside him is an army of Shadow Beast called the Drakere. They can take over your mind and soul, and no one would know unless it deemed it so. The army is full of man-like beasts that stand taller than us." Fear shot across the crowd, and the weeping cries of children were being comforted with the warm bosoms of their mothers.

"I will fight." A young man, around the same age as Abbygale, stepped forward. "If you ask for us to bear arms and fight for you. Then I will do it." Many more followed the young man's lead. "Where will our families stay while we go to war?"

"We have a cave that is protected by dragon magic.

No evil can see it. Those who do not wish to fight or are unable will be safe there with the children." I said with pride in my voice. "I thank you for your loyalty and will be honored to fight with my fellow countrymen."

The crowd dispersed to pack for the journey to the Ice Cave.

"That was some speech you gave, Sis."

"Is that a compliment I hear?"

"I love you with all my heart. Whatever happens on the battlefield, I will have your back."

"We will be fine. We will save Mother and our people. We will avenge Tristian."

****

Rowland

The frosty night air reminded me of the first time entering this unfamiliar land. The crispy breeze, loud crunching beneath my feet, and an aroma of nature that was, in comparison, more pleasing than those of Zoldir. I'm not sure I ever want to go back because that would mean leaving her. And that is something I'll never do again. In the distance, I notice Kaleigh speaking with Azula. Her beautiful brown hair, fastened in two braids, complimented her well-mannered physique.

When everyone settled in for the evening, I found myself sitting behind Kaleigh in a steaming bath in a private room we were given in the village inn. Her body fit perfectly against mine as I rubbed her shoulder while she rested her head back against my chest. The lavender soap and the feel of her naked skin pressing against mine was like taking an aphrodisiac. When my hand drifted to her clit, I teased it every so slightly to catch her attention.

She didn't move. I started rubbing it gently with

one hand while the other palmed her left breast. Her nipples hardened and she moaned. I inserted two fingers and pumped them in and out while continuing to bring out her first orgasm. I sunk my teeth into her shoulder, tightening my hold as she began to ride my fingers.

"Rowland, fuck me." She moaned and I increased my pace until I felt her clench down. I didn't wait. My cock was ready for her. I gripped her hips, lifted her, and plunge my cock deep inside of her making the water splash. I didn't care that we were flooding the floor.

Chapter Twenty-Six

Kaleigh

If there was anything that this man could do right, it was fuck me until I was seeing starlight. His grip on my hips told me I'd have bruises tomorrow but I didn't care. I palmed my breast and began rubbing my clit as we locked lips over my shoulder. Our tongues danced and I moaned when he took one hand and moved it to my asshole.

"I've never–"

"Don't worry, princess. I'll make sure it feels good but we need to move this to the bed." I nodded and we got out of the tub. We didn't even dry off because we knew tonight might be our last chance. Our last moment to be together because tomorrow war would be upon us and there was no guarantee any of us would remain alive.

My back pressed into the cloth linen as I grip his cock tip to shaft while he kissed me. Last time, our souls connected and we finally accepted one another as soul mates. He was mine and I was his for all time. There isn't anything I wouldn't do for him.

"I need to prep you, princess."

He got off the bed and walked over to his bag grabbing something out before coming back. "This gel will help ease the pain. I'm going to make to cum all over my cock before I claim your ass."

I blushed and bit my lip.

His fingers were coated in the liquid and it felt cold against my bum. My body was hot. I could feel my heart thundering and my pussy getting wetter as he toyed with me. His mouth was on my clit He licked and sucked and started pushing the tip of one finger in and out slowly. I gripped his hair and started to lift my hips. "Ride my face, princess. It will make it feel better with my fingers prepping your ass for my cock."

"Rowland." My voice came out breathlessly as I felt him go all the way to his knuckle and started adding the tip of the other finger. His pace was quickening, matching my rhythm as I chased my orgasm on his tongue. "Please. More."

I couldn't form sentences. But I needed him. All of him.

"Rowland, fuck me!" The second finger went in and he gave me a punishing pace that burned and stretched but mixed with the pleasure of his tongue had me on the edge.

I couldn't hold on any longer. My thighs closed tightly around his head as I screamed his name in ecstasy.

"Are you ready, princess?"

"Now," I demanded as I gripped his tip and lined it up with my entrance. "Claim me." I flipped over on my belly. The anticipation and thought of what this was going to be like had my hands roaming over my body. I pinched my nipples as he started to push. My clit was sensitive but I needed more. I pushed back against him hard and screamed, as he went all the way into the hilt.

"Breathe," he commanded as I looked over my

shoulder at him.

"Fast, Rowland. Hard. That's what I want. What I need. Can you give me that?"

He smirked, claiming my lips, and without saying another word, gripped the back of my neck in my hand and my hip in the other and fucked me.

It was as if I unlocked this fire in him. He wouldn't let me look away, gripping my wrist, forcing them behind my back. I thought I was going to fall over but his cock was locked deep inside of my ass.

"I'm not stopping until my cum fills all of your holes tonight, princess. Dripping from your pussy."He inserted two fingers, making me clench then pulled them out. "This pretty little mouth." He pushed those inside and I could taste our mixed arousals. "Don't worry, princess, I'll be clean before I take you here. I want you gagging on me, begging for breath. My seed is going to look so good on you."

"Fuck!" I moaned.

I was on the verge of another orgasm. He pinched my nipple and that sent me over but he kissed me, muffling it and then I felt him. He quickened again, then slowed as his cock expanded inside of me. I could feel his hot seed spilling before we fell over. Taking a moment to breathe, he slowly pulled out.

Rowland wasn't done with me. I watched him quickly get up, bathe his entire body while I got some water, and then came prowling at me without drying off. My mouth watered and I was jealous of every droplet coating his delectable skin. I got to my knees before him and didn't wait. I licked slowly the shaft at first. Then sucked each ball into my mouth while rubbing him. When he was hard once more, I looked at him as he gripped my hair and said, "Open."

His tip hit the back of my throat in one thrust.

He wasn't slow or soft. I had no control, which is what I needed. What I wanted. I was gagging, trying to keep up by swallowing and he groaned and panted with each thrust. I reached up and rubbed his balls with one hand while the other explored his ass. I moved it to his taint and played while he fucked my mouth. I could feel my eyes water and then, his hot seed spilled down my throat.

When he pulled out, he lifted me into his arms and laid us on the soaked sheets. I couldn't move. He wrapped me in his arms tightly and I kissed him softly before saying, "Thank you for letting me lose control. For giving me your heart. I love you, Rowland Kawthrone and I can't wait to marry you."

Chapter Twenty-Seven

Rowland

I awoke to my beautiful fiancée bouncing up and down on my cock. Her breasts enticing me to mark them."Wake up. I need you to fuck me before we leave but we need to quick."

She was breathtaking and I let her remain in control as I pumped her with my seed. A vision of her with a round belly had me falling even deeper in love. "When you're with child, I'll have to restrain myself more, although I'm not sure I'll be able to."

"Rowland," she moaned and kissed me as we both went into bliss once more before leaving for war.

****

Entering the village square again, the busy nature of everyone gave a sense of urgency to me. Azula and Verglas were far away. Abby gestured to the children and adults who wished not to fight in one area while Kaleigh gathered all the villagers, ready to die for her.

"Now remember, once we start, there is no coming back until we have won." Kaleigh was giving a pep talk to less than fifty villagers. Each was armed with various weapons. "I know you think your pitchforks, cutlery, and hammers are not much to fight with, but you gain a more adequate weapon with each enemy you kill. I will lead the armies in the front, while my sister will join us with reinforcements once those seeking shelter are safe. If you wish to say goodbye, now is your last opportunity. We move out in ten minutes."

The crowd dispersed to find their children to give what might be their last hug.

The journey down the stone path would take a day and a half with as many people as they gathered. A diverse group of men and women. Each willing to fight and die for their princess and country. Kaleigh had a way of motivating people with her words. It's one of the things I've come to realize is what made me fall for her.

"Is this your first fight, sir?" To my right is an older gentleman with silver hair, a hunched back, and misty eyes that brought him out of his current state of tunnel vision.

"Sorry to say it isn't," I responded.

"I'm glad that a skilled warrior will fight on the same side as us. Why do you think the king from the other side did it?"

"Did what?"

"Well, help the dark sorcerer invade and take over the fortress."

"I'm sure everyone has their reasons for doing things. It may seem right to them, but to others, it is wrong."

"He is wrong, your brother. He is a wicked man." The man's voice changed.

"What did you just say to me?"

"I said, this king will get what's coming to him. What he is doing. It isn't right." I stopped in my tracks. Confused and wondering if my mind was playing tricks on me. I am going crazy. Seeing things, hearing things that are not there.

"Is everything all right?"

"Yes."

"You look like you're going to be sick."

****

"Princess," said the young woman walking beside me, dressed in a brown, tattered dress with small holes in various places. "Do you think we are going to win?" her brown hair was matted, with pieces of leaves nestled between her fine hairs. A mouth of brown teeth, with foul breath and a dirty pale face, eagerly awaits an answer. It almost made me cringe in fear.

"I will be right on the front lines. Going sword first to ensure we win the battle. I cannot promise no death or injury, but I can promise I will not stop until our land and our people are safe from the evil that threatens it." The young girl's dull smile and a look of reassurance warmed my heart, knowing I brought some ease to one of her citizens.

This village is entirely of people just like her. How come Father never helped them? I stopped the herd approaching the border edge between Snow Forest and Orion Market. "We need to send out a scouting party. We do not know the seriousness of the situation beyond the border. I need a volunteer to join me." Looking around, no hand was raised; no voice was heard above the quietness of the crowd. "Very well. I need you all to make camp and wait for my return."

The timid crowd of villagers dispersed and prepared a temporary campsite. I ensured I had my sword and enough rations for a day or two.

"May I volunteer to join you?" Rowland asked.

"I need someone to stay here with the villagers," I

said.

"I told you last night we would never be apart again and I meant that, princess." His voice's heightened tone of frustration and heated look in his amber eyes told me just how serious he was

"Who will look after the villagers? These people aren't skilled fighters or trackers. They need someone to lead them."

"I can do that," Abby said stepping up. "No need for you two lovebirds to get separated and repeat the endless cycle that has been the last six months." Neither of us was sure what she meant. She sighed. "You get captured, she rescues you, and vice versa. It's a nauseating love story if you ask me."

"Only if you're sure," I asked, and when she nodded, I didn't question it. Because at that moment, I knew my little sister no longer needed me to protect her.

The marbled stone path covered in snow quickly turned into a dark path full of debris. Missing stones left holes in the bridge that crossed over into the market square. My heart was filled with sorrow at the disastrous scene.

Flickering flames from a fiery assault hung over the leftovers of the once-great market.

"What... what happened here?" The surprise in my voice rang through my ears. "Where is everyone?" just as I said, a crunching sound came from underneath their feet.

"Oh, my...." The charred, screaming faces of burned bodies lay on the blackened ground. A crushed, tiny hand of a little girl reached out toward the burned body of her mother. "All these innocent people, all those buildings. This wasn't just an attack. This was pure cold-blooded murder."

"We need to keep moving." Rowland gripped my hand and ushered me forward as we both kept looking around for any sign of life. Good or bad.

"What else is there to see? This is what we are up against. All these people lost their lives and their homes. They didn't even have time to leave." The anger in my voice was equally matched with the rage that every bone in my body felt.

"We need to get an idea of their numbers."

The smell of burned flesh clung within my nose like flies to horse dung. The cracked stones of the once beautiful pathways saddened my already vengeful heart. A place I once called home, covered in the blood and bones of the innocent. Our pace quickens the closer we get to the fortress.

Not a single torch or guard in sight. What are you playing at Santana? The eerie feeling in the air sends shivers down my spine. A fortitude of strength and loyalty brought down by betrayal. Sneaking my way into the servant's entrance, there must be at least one loyal person. Dark and empty. What is that smell? The foul stench of rotten flesh wafted through the frigid air.

****

Rowland

"Where is the Princess?"

"Why isn't she with you?" many questions had him rush over to see what all the commotion was about.

"Katrina?" She was standing there, out of breath, black soot and blood covering her entire body. "Where is she? Why do you have blood and ash on you?" his heart paced with the fear of unwelcome news.

"I couldn't stop her. She would not listen to me. Rowland, I am sorry, but... she is gone." Katrina's words echoed in his head over and over. Gone? But how? There is no way, Verglas said... *"Rowland, Rowland, sweetie."*

"Mother?" his eyes wandered around. *"What happened? Where am I?"*

"Calm down. You hit your head really hard." Looking around, confused at the sight of his own mother.

"How did I get back home? How are you here?" A look of confusion ran across her smooth, pale face.

"You must have hit your head much harder than we expected."

"No," jumping out of his bed, *"this isn't possible. I was there. It was real."*

"What was real? Your dream?"

"Who are you? Santana, you are powerful, but you cannot deceive me. I have the gift of sight." Bursting out in laughter, the beautiful image of his mother turned into the despicable, dark picture of the evil emperor.

"You are a smart one." Clapping his hands to tease him. I saw his sword perched up against the wall. Reaching for it, only to have it disappear right before him. *"If your mother wasn't real, do you honestly think that would have been real too?"*

"You better be happy it wasn't real because if it was..."

"You would have what?" she interrupted. *"Rowland, I would like to offer you a deal."* The rage grew inside of him. *"Oh, just sit down and listen."* With a wave of his hand, Santana forced me to sit in a chair.

235

"Now, I know your dear Princess is in my new kingdom, desperately trying to save everyone. But I will have her in my prison soon enough." This made me jerk in my chair.

"You see that passion right there; that is exactly why I am here." That devilish black smile came across his face. *"I will let your Princess go undetected if you are my little spy."*

"What makes you think I will help you?"

"Because your dear brother did. And if you do not, let us say the princess will be in my bed chambers, and your brother will be dragon food." I felt my heart sink. *"Now you see it. You have a choice to make, Rowland. Become my spy and save the love of your life and idiot brother. Or watch me rape her and feed your brother to Xiong."*

Snapping awake, I found myself asleep next to a fire. It was all just a dream. Quickly getting to my feet I look for her, "Where is Kaleigh?"

"Over there," I didn't realize I was alone when my thoughts slipped out. I turned around to find a guard chained to a wall next to us. I moved to get to her, but I was jerked backward by my chains. How did we end up here? A noise came from her as she rubbed the back of her head when sitting up.

"Rowland? What happened? We were making our way inside when I blacked out." She looked around then her eyes locked onto mine. "How did we get in the dungeons?"

"I'm not sure. But I think Katrina betrayed us somehow. We both blacked out and I had a vision. What about you?"

"No." Her voice was soft and she looked to the

floor. "No! No! No!" Her chains rattled as her head fell into her lap and shoulders shook with her tears. "I failed them. I failed everyone."

"No, you didn't, princess." I wanted to reach out to her. To hold her tightly. "Look at me, princess. For the love of everything right in this world, I need you to do that." When she lifted her tear-soaked face, it enraged me. "We're in this together, forever no matter what. So if you failed, I failed. And I'm the worse of the two because it means I failed you."

"I love you," she whispered.

"Do you remember what Feanor said about you?" She shook her head from side to side. "Well I do. You have the heart of a warrior, the mind and strength of the gods, and you are the savior. There is nothing that can stop you because you're Kaleigh Orion, queen of this fortress, my soul mate, and there is nothing that can stop you."

When my words finished, the room was deadly quiet.

Then, in her hand, glowing bright as the sapphire color of her eyes, was the stone. Her chains were coated in ice and when she jerked her arms forward, they shattered into pieces.

"How? I don't have magic," she exclaimed.

"We should talk about this with Verglas later," I said as she rushed over to free me and the other prisoner.

Chapter Twenty-Eight

Kaleigh

Dead carcasses spread out all over the palace floors. The mix of human remains and Humanoid Soldiers. My brown leather boot was covered in the blood and guts of what used to be the Chef. Chef, I am so sorry this happened to you. I pulled my shirt over my nose as she exited the trashed servant's quarters. I stopped as she overheard the loud stepping sounds of hooves.

"Find her. He knows she is in here somewhere. And if you do, bring her straight to me alive."

That is no beast talking. I know that voice. Peeking around the corner, my eyes widened, heart fluttered, and a smile came across my face as I gazed upon him. Silver hair tied back. All black clothes from torso to foot. Tristian? Debating on whether I should reveal my position, I watch further. Half-hoping this was real and the other hoping if it was real, Tristian was still on her side.

"That's not him, princess," Rowland whispered in my ear.

"Then it must be Santana."

Waiting until the guards passed, we turned the corner following him. The halls of her home are strange to her. The tapestries have all changed their color, black with gold lacey. At the center, a pentagram with a black stone at the center. Iron steel torches set an ambiance that is both gloomy and sinister. Entering through a larch stone archway, I was greeted with a familiar aroma of rosemary.

The Willow Well Garden. It is the only piece left intact since the takeover. Mesmerized by the warmth the garden brings me, I didn't realize Tristian was no longer in my sights. I wonder why you were left untouched. Oh, how I have missed you! My place of peace and serenity. Sitting next to the water, I hum as I run my fingers through the cold liquid.

"I was wondering when you would come back?" I do not budge at the sound of his voice. "You can't even hear me, can you?"His fingers snap next to my ear, "I say the spell worked. What you see, my dear princess, is your once beautiful garden." He paused. "But what you do not see is the ash left over from the botanicals, and you are not running your fingers through water. No." He leans down to whisper in her ears, "You are running your fingers through the blood of your mother and father."

Tristian's voice echoes in my head. I break the trance and desperately look around as the world changes.

"Tristian? Is it really you? Where is he? Where is Rowland?"

"You see your beast friend and former fuck buddy for the first time in three months and you're more concerned about the enemy prince?" He feigned heartbreak. I didn't care because I knew in my heart this wasn't him. "I was dead. Abby stayed loyal to me but you. When I found out from the leaders down there,"—he pointed to the ground because we all believe that is the realm where our souls go to when we die—"told me you were fucking the prince, man, was I pissed."

"You were with my sister, why did it matter to you?" I was stalling until Rowland could come or figure out where he was.

"That was just a coy to make you jealous. To make you realize what you were missing out on. I loved the sweet taste of her virgin cunt and the feel of it wrapped around my cunt but you know what I loved the most?" He paused and I drew the hidden dagger from my back. I calmed my breathing, focusing on his chest as he spoke the last words I'd ever want to hear from him again. "She was on her knees. Mouth opened wide and I fu–"

His eyes widened. Mouth agape as black liquid seeped out of him. "How?"

"Didn't you read up on ghostly lore? Ice made from white magic can kill those made from dark. You're not the real Tristian. And if you are, I never really knew you."

I twisted the jagged edge deep inside, backing off and leaving it. I watched in amazement and glee as his body turned from ice to stone before shattering to pieces. "

****

Rowland

Sweat dripped, mixing with the blood splatters across my face. The attack came out of nowhere. I lost Kaleigh in the heat of it but Abby quickly came with an army of elves and villagers. I'm not sure how she did it, but we had enough numbers now to win this.

The taste of salty iron seeps into my mouth. During a deadly battle for life and freedom. Swinging, stabbing, and slaying our enemies with all my strength. There are too many of them. I dreamed of being a knight in a real war but now I see just how foolish that was. *Verglas, if you can hear me, hurry.* Screams of terror and death encircle him.

"Abby! Abby, where are you?" I shouted, knowing that if I let her die, Kaleigh would never forgive me.

"You like that." Through the dust and smoke, the tiny figure of Abby going head-to-head with a beast entices me to run to her rescue. Raising my sword, I thrust it into its back, forcing a dying howl out of his mouth. "I didn't ask for your help."

"Well, if you die, Kaleigh will kill me."

"Wow." She rolled her eyes.

"What? What did I say?" Abby tackled me to the ground just as Leijon's fire rained down from above. "I didn't ask you to help."

"Yes, well, she will kill us both if either of us dies." Helping me to my feet, she says, "Follow me. I know the way in."

"We have to get to your sister before Santana does. She's the key to winning this." I figured that out the moment she controlled that stone.

Leading me through a side entrance to the castle, the remains of a wooden door clung to its hinges.

"Where does this lead?"

"This was the servant's entrance. Chef?" We stumbled upon the rotting head of the palace Chef. Fear of death still lingers in his eyes. "When we find him, I am going to kill him."

Running down the darkened corridors, avoiding

each battle between man and beast, I ask Abby, "Where do you think she is?"

"My best guess would be the throne room. And if he is there, Kaleigh is too." We soon approach the massive doors that lead inside. "No guards. Why isn't it guarded?"

"Probably because we are in the middle of a war," I whisper.

"No shit." We moved forward. "I will go in first."

I grabbed her waist, pushed her against the wall, covered her mouth, and said, "I am going first. You will wait for me to say go because if my brother, Kaleigh, and that evil bastard are in there, I won't be killed on site. You will be used as leverage. I will let you go, but you must agree to stay here." Abby nods and, just as I'm releasing her, knees me in the groin.

"You don't get to tell me what to do." She pushes me to the ground and runs inside. Why doesn't she like me? I am so thankful I do not have a sister. I painfully get to my feet and run inside. Abby is standing, frozen like a statue. "Rowland, stop! It's a trap." Kaleigh was fighting against a forcefield and directly behind it, the last person I expected to see was holding a dagger to her throat. "He used the stone."

"We meet again, Rowland." Santana came out of nowhere, caressing the blue stone in his fingers. "White magic is so weak, the slightest influence of darkness can make its' will bend to my command."

"Let them go," I growled.

"Rowland," Gregor called my name. "Kaleigh will never be yours. You will never get to feel the moist, ardent passion of her body against yours ever again." My heart cracks. Knees buckle. And sword clatters to the floor as his dagger pierces her beautiful flesh.

"I warned you of what would happen, young Lord." Santana sighs, patting my head. My hands hit the cold stone floor and curl. There was nothing I felt aside from the increasing rage. It was like a forest fire with a limitless amount of fuel. Nothing to stop it from burning this world to the ground.

I felt the curved blade of Santana's ax at the back of my neck."Good-bye, brother."

Gregor's hardened voice lit the final fuse as fire erupted from my throat burning the emperor and causing him to drop his weapon. I don't know how or why, but I wasn't going to stop tapping into this power.

My nails turned into talons. I dug those deep into Santana's chest until I could feel the beating of his black heart. The last thing witnessed was his still beating organ gripped in my hand. I then turned my focus on Gregor.

"You killed her. There is nothing that will save you." I pushed through the forcefield. His eyes moved but his body was cemented in place. I knew in that moment, my brother was gone. Taken over by a drakere. I watched as his body slowly turned to ash.

I fell to my knees, cradling her in my arms.

"Rowland," she croaked, and I smiled at the sound of my name.

"I'm here, princess."

"Kiss me." I pressed my lips to hers. A loud roar came from the windows just before Azula burst through them.

"Rowland, bring her here. Quickly, *now*." I held her hand while Azula sniffed her. "I can save her but it will take a spell. And it will be painful. I need your help."

"There isn't anything I wouldn't do for her," I said.

"Lay down next to her. Hold her hand tightly and no matter what you feel, what you see and or hear, do not let go. Do you understand me? It is vital." I nod and did as I was told. Azula reached the tip of her talon to my chest and began to whisper in a language I didn't comprehend. I didn't feel anything at first.

It started slowly. Like my skin was scratched by a thorn. Then that pain grew into a stabbing pain as if her talon dug deeper until I saw it. My heart was beating out of my chest. It burned until half of it because ice and broken off. Azula chanted more magical words and touched me. This time it felt like my body was ice. I couldn't move. No thoughts came to mind as I was paralyzed where I lay.

"Close your eyes, Rowland. Heal her with your love. With your soul."

I saw her clear as day standing in front of me. Her belly round with twins. A boy and a girl. She smiled at me and I saw a small scar in the shape of an arrow over her chest and then looked down at mine in the same spot. I had one to match.

I captured her lips. Pouring every moment, every memory, every dream, and every wish for us into her. It was a cup that never stopped flowing.

"Rowland?" I opened my eyes at the sound of her voice.

I pulled her into my arms. "I thought I lost you."

"You two now share a single heart," Azula said. "If one of you dies, so does the other."

"That's how it should be," I said."

"What about my sister?" Kaleigh asked as we

walked up to her statue. "She's frozen solid."

Azula let out a roar of hot breath and the ice soon melted.

"What the fuck just happened?" Abby asked as she rubbed her arms. "And why is it so cold?"

We laughed, telling her what happened, and then embraced each other as a family.

"What now?" Abby said as she laid her weary head across Kaleigh's lap.

"Now, we reunite Dalaria."

A word about the author…

C. M. Hano is a Fantasy Romance Author who aspires to write strong female-driven, hot, and magical adventures, and be a good mother. She lives in Louisiana with her husband and three beautiful children.

Thank you for purchasing
this publication of The Wild Rose Press, Inc.

For questions or more information
contact us at
info@thewildrosepress.com.

The Wild Rose Press, Inc.
www.thewildrosepress.com